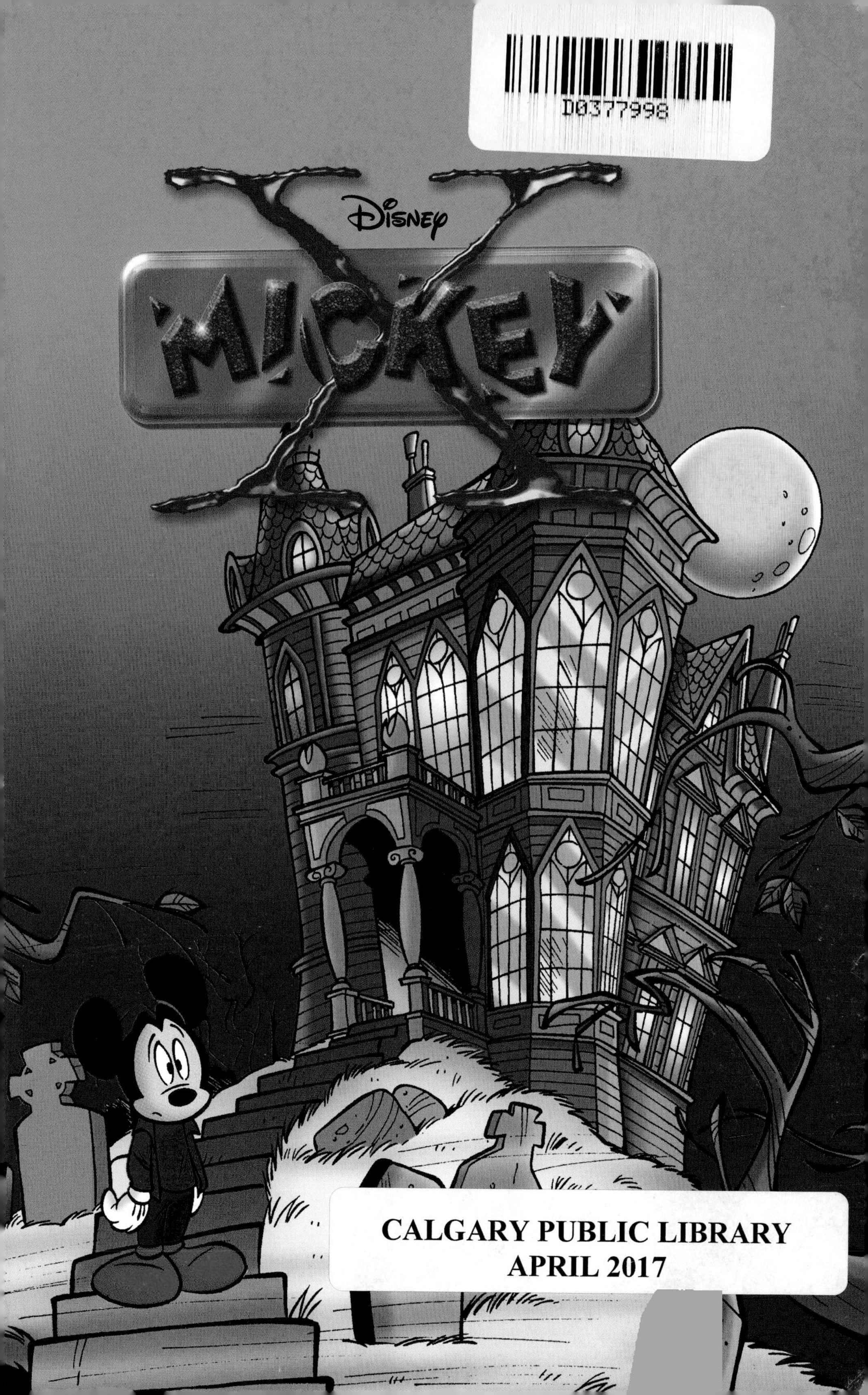
Disney
X
MICKEY

Disney Graphic Novels available from PAPERCUTZ

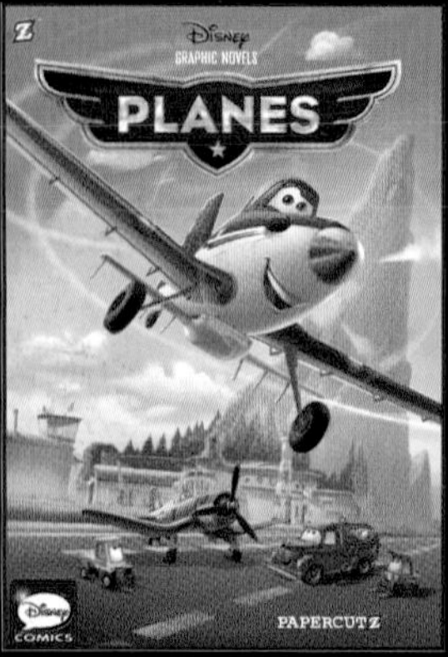
Disney
GRAPHIC NOVELS
PLANES
PAPERCUTZ
DISNEY PLANES

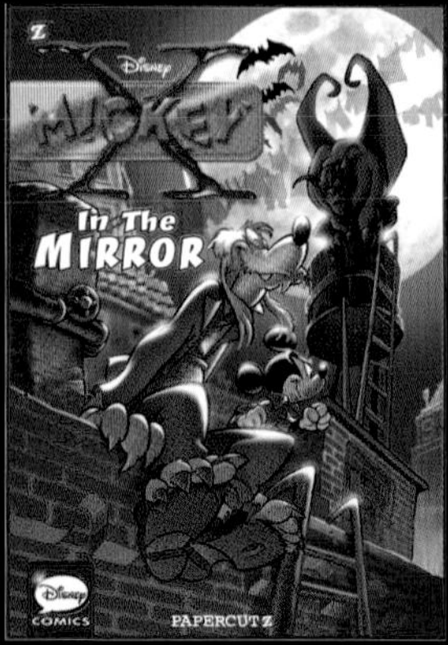
Disney
X MICKEY
In The MIRROR
PAPERCUTZ
DISNEY X-MICKEY #1

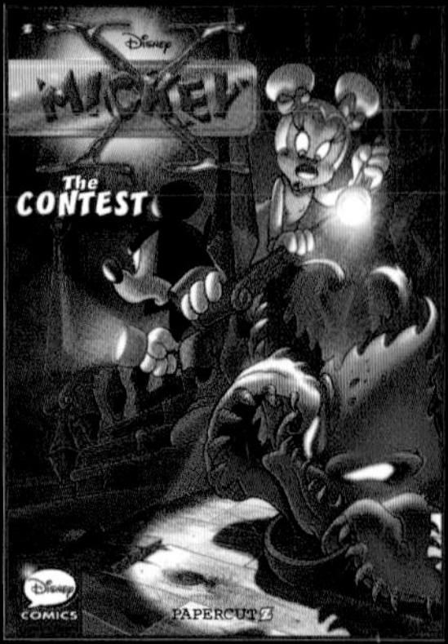
Disney
X MICKEY
The CONTEST
PAPERCUTZ
DISNEY X-MICKEY #2

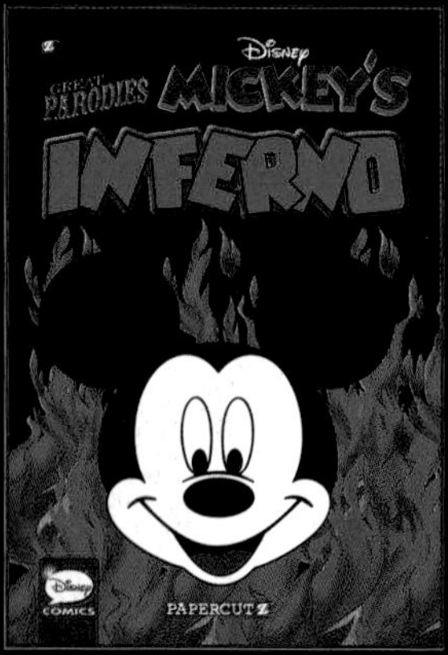
Disney
GREAT PARODIES
MICKEY'S INFERNO
PAPERCUTZ
MICKEY'S INFERNO

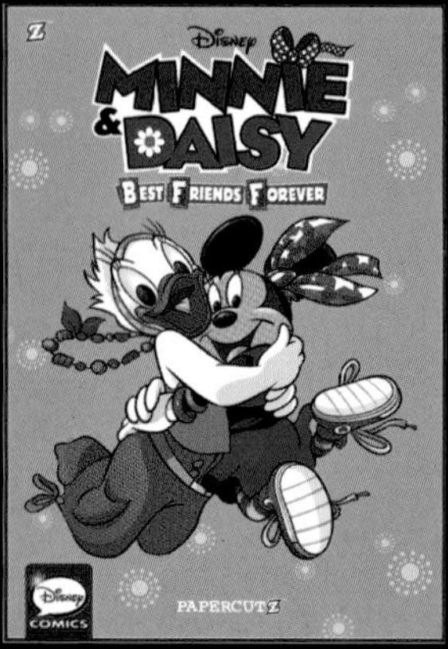
Disney
MINNIE & DAISY
BEST FRIENDS FOREVER
PAPERCUTZ
DISNEY MINNIE & DAISY BFF #1

COMING SOON

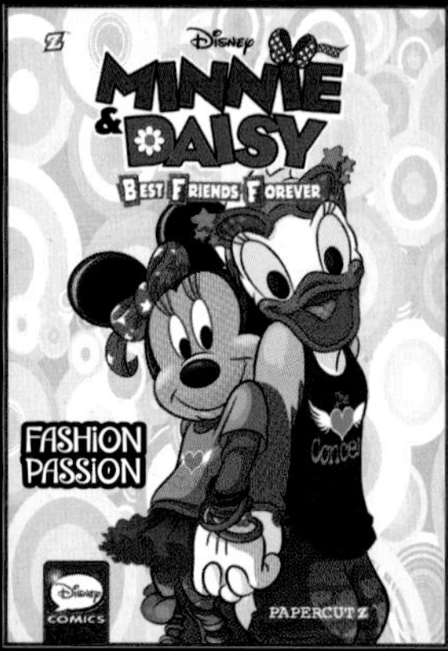
Disney
MINNIE & DAISY
BEST FRIENDS FOREVER
FASHION PASSION
PAPERCUTZ
DISNEY MINNIE & DAISY #2

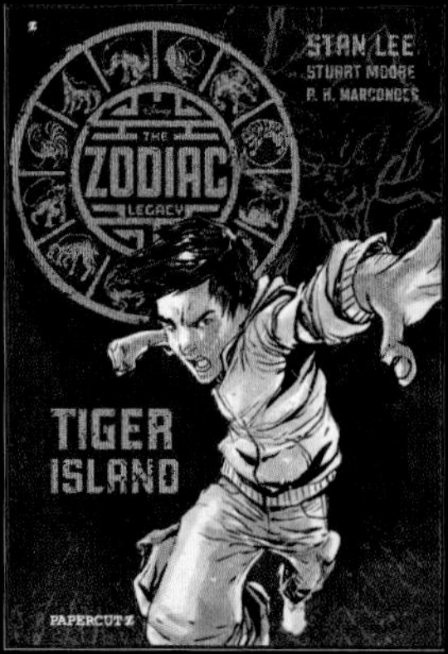
STAN LEE
STUART MOORE
P. H. MARCONDES
THE ZODIAC LEGACY
TIGER ISLAND
PAPERCUTZ
DISNEY THE ZODIAC LEGACY #1

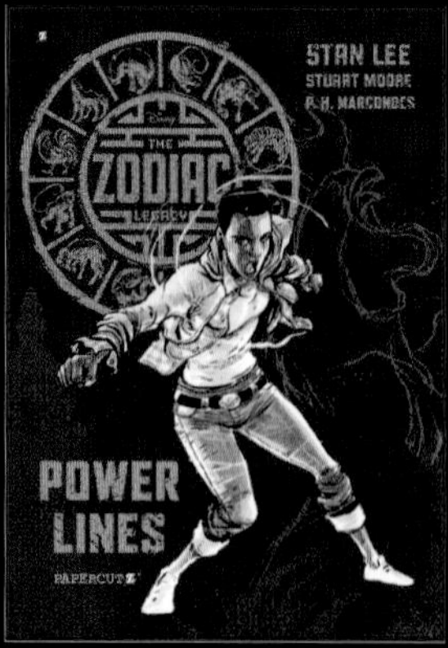
STAN LEE
STUART MOORE
P. H. MARCONDES
THE ZODIAC LEGACY
POWER LINES
PAPERCUTZ
DISNEY THE ZODIAC LEGACY #2

COMING SOON

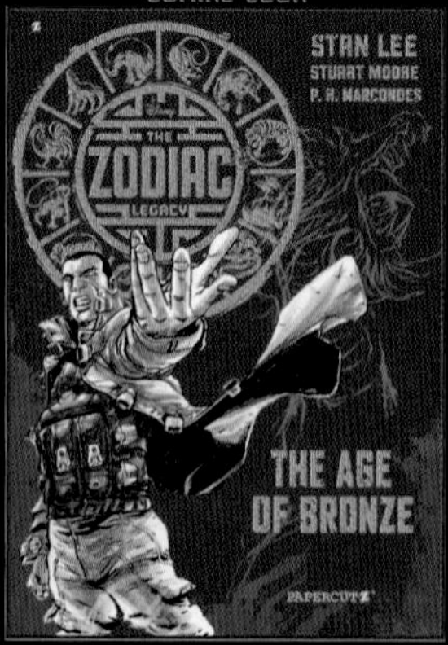
STAN LEE
STUART MOORE
P. H. MARCONDES
THE ZODIAC LEGACY
THE AGE OF BRONZE
PAPERCUTZ
DISNEY THE ZODIAC LEGACY #3

Disney graphic novels are available in paperback for $7.99 each; in hardcover for $12.99 each. MICKEY'S INFERNO is available in paperback for $8.99 each and in hardcover for $13.99 each. Available at booksellers everywhere. Or you can order from us: Please add $4.00 for postage and handling for first book, and add $1.00 for each additional book. Please make check payable to NBM Publishing. Send to: Papercutz, 160 Broadway, Suite 700, East Wing, New York, NY 10038 or call 800-886-1223 (9-6 EST M-F) MC-Visa-Amex accepted

Disney

Mickey X

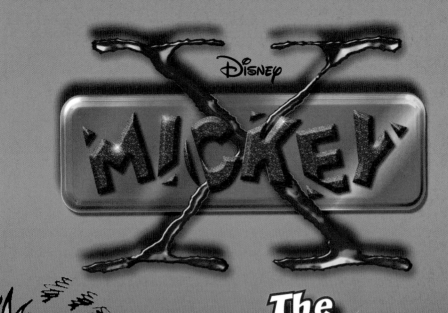

The Contest

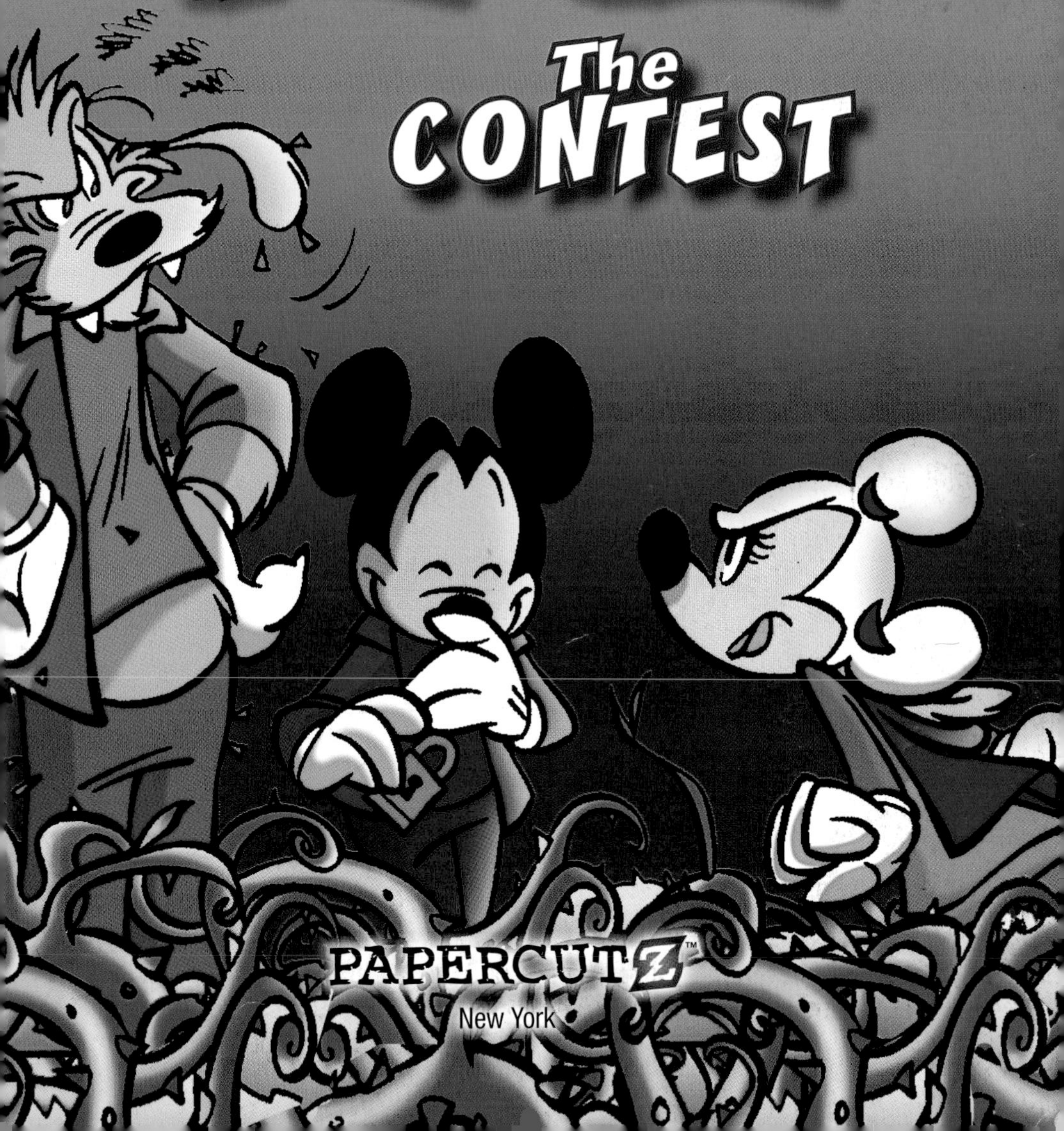

PAPERCUTZ™

New York

CONTENTS

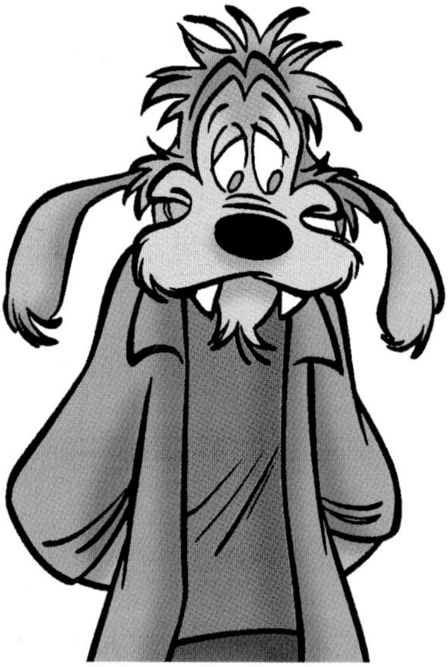

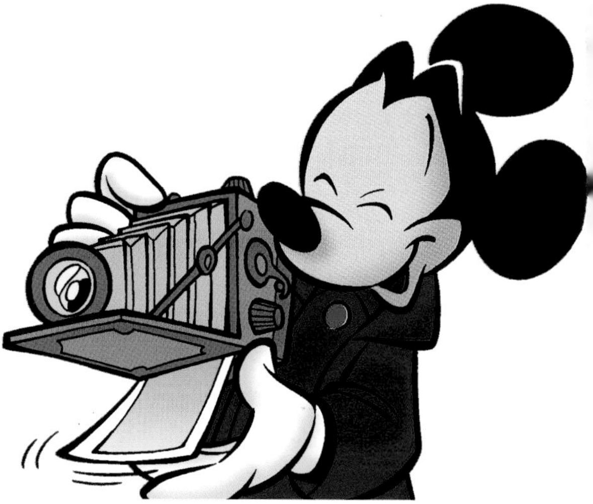

DISNEY GRAPHIC NOVELS #5
MICKEY
"THE CONTEST"

Stefano Ambrosio – Writer
Stefano Intini – Artist
Dawn K. Guzzo – Design and Production
Sasha Kimiatek – Production Coordinator
Robert V. Conte – Editor
Jeff Whitman – Assistant Managing Editor
Jim Salicrup
Editor-in-Chief

Special Thanks – Carlotta Quattrocolo, Arianna Marchione,
[illegible] and Eugene Paraszczuk at Disney Enterprises, Inc.

ISBN: [illegible] Paperback Edition
ISBN: [illegible] Hardcover Edition

Printed in Korea through Four Colour Print Group Ltd.
[illegible]

Distributed by Macmillan
First Papercutz Printing

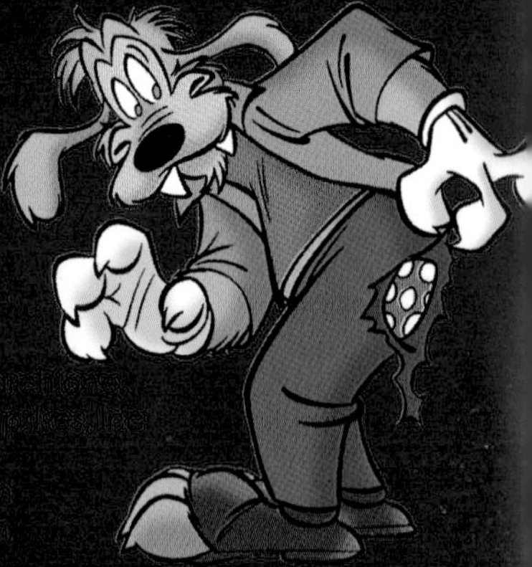

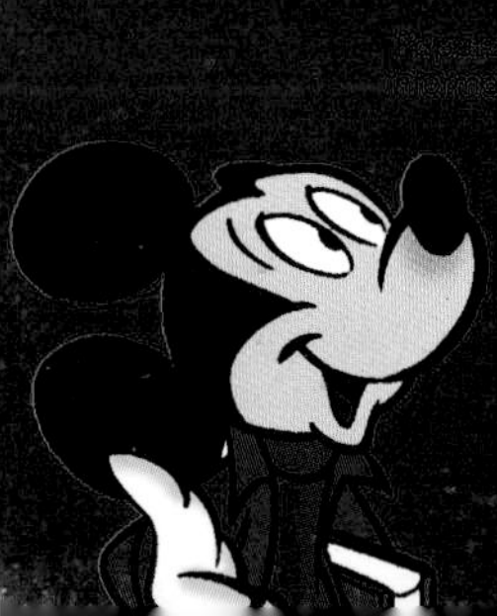

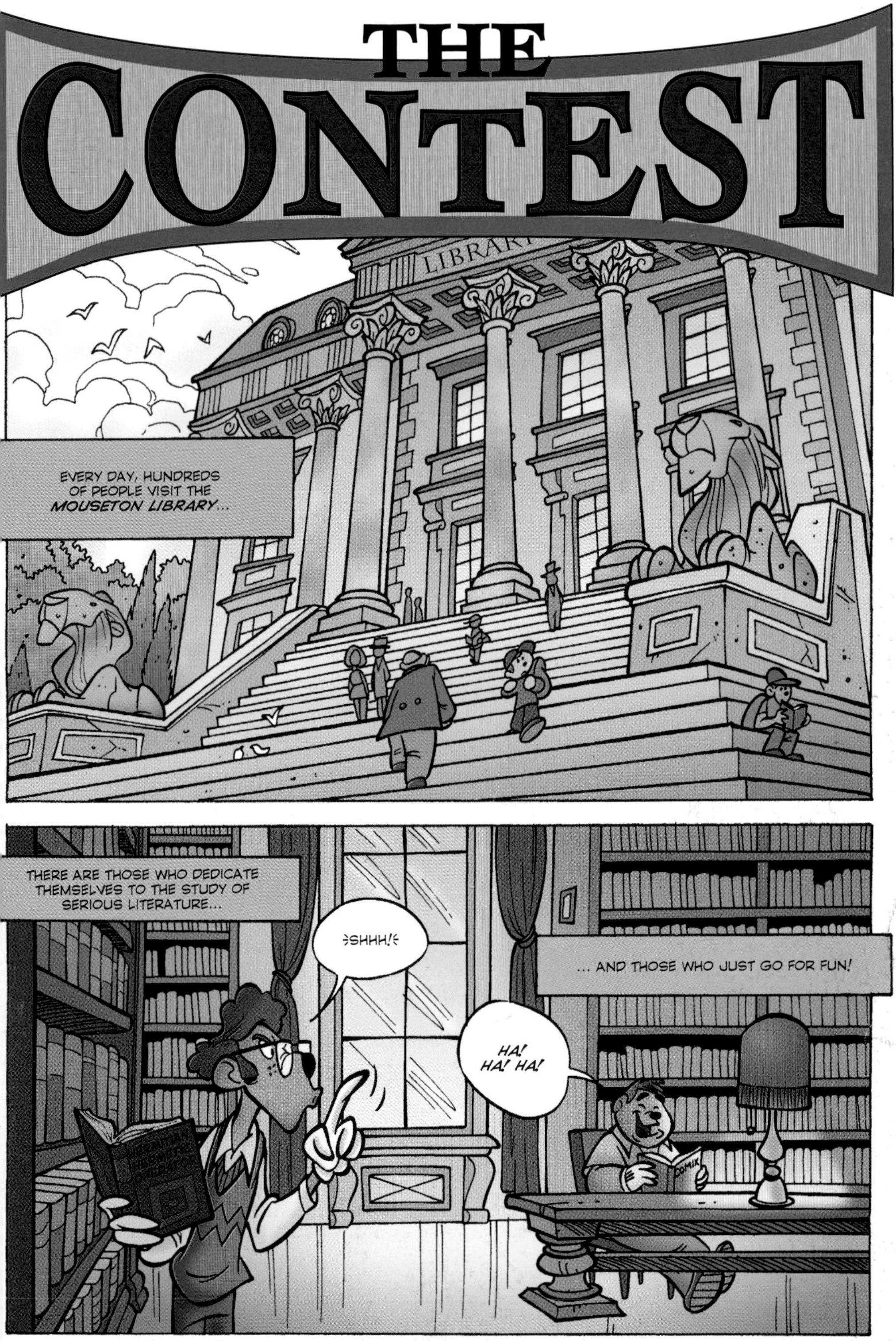
THE CONTEST
EVERY DAY, HUNDREDS OF PEOPLE VISIT THE *MOUSETON LIBRARY*...
THERE ARE THOSE WHO DEDICATE THEMSELVES TO THE STUDY OF SERIOUS LITERATURE...
SHHH!
... AND THOSE WHO JUST GO FOR FUN!
HA! HA! HA!
COMIX

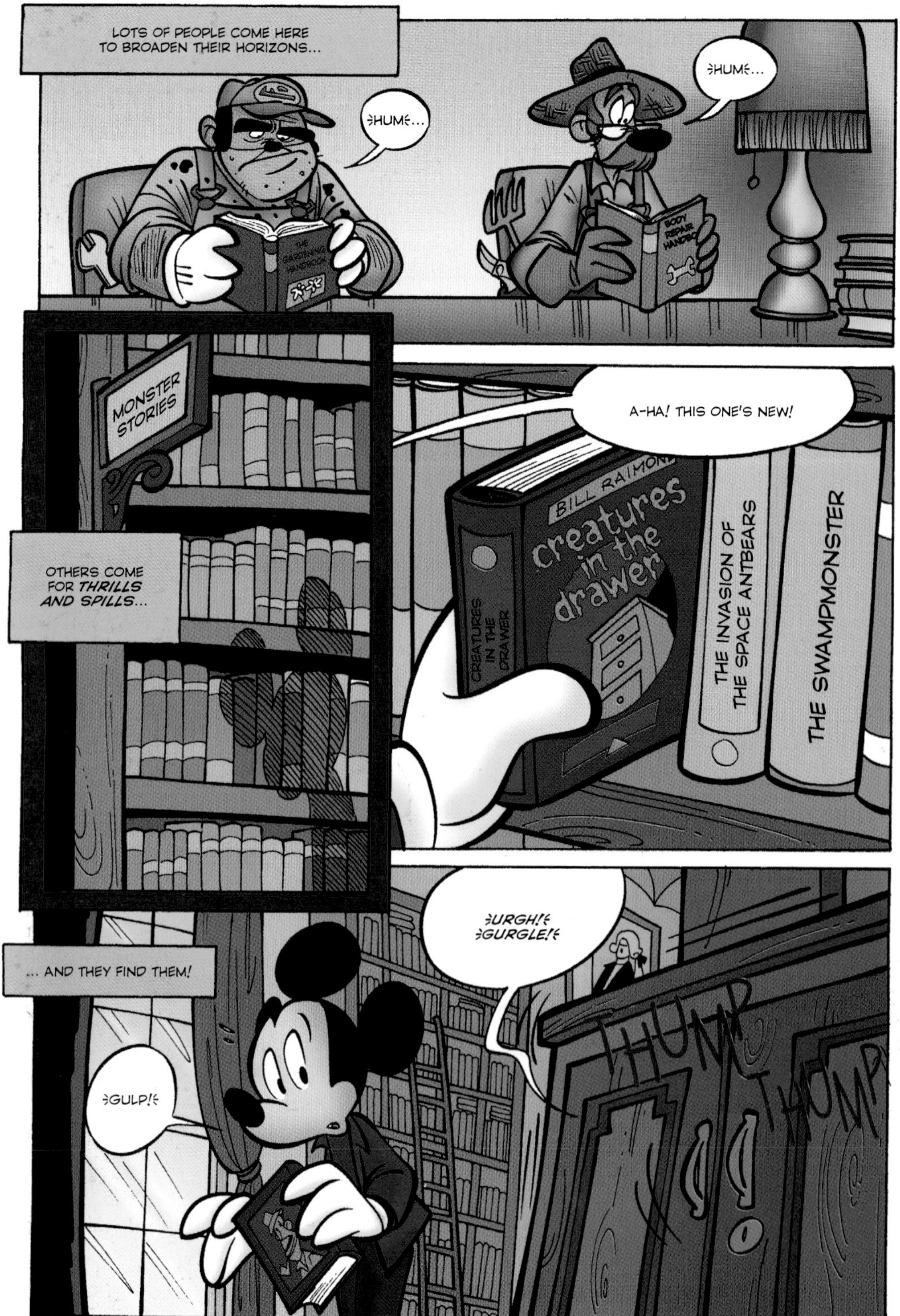
LOTS OF PEOPLE COME HERE
TO BROADEN THEIR HORIZONS...
HUM...
THE GARDENING HANDBOOK
HUM...
BODY REPAIR HANDBOOK
MONSTER STORIES
OTHERS COME
FOR THRILLS
AND SPILLS...
A-HA! THIS ONE'S NEW!
BILL RAIMON
creatures in the drawer
CREATURES IN THE DRAWER
THE INVASION OF THE SPACE ANTBEARS
THE SWAMPMONSTER
... AND THEY FIND THEM!
URGH!
GURGLE!
GULP!
THUMP
THUMP

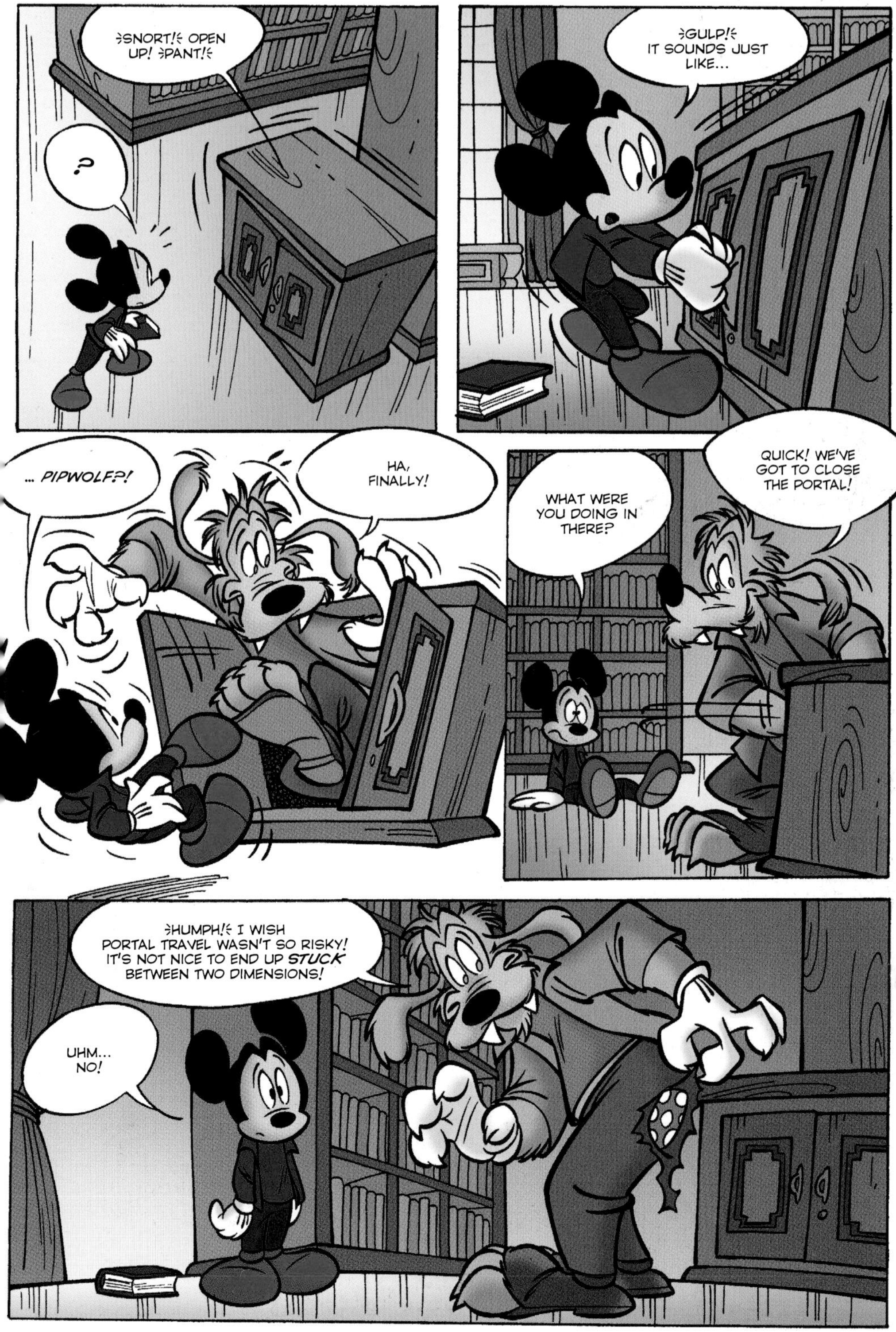

⁝SNORT!⁝ OPEN UP! ⁝PANT!⁝
?
⁝GULP!⁝ IT SOUNDS JUST LIKE...
... PIPWOLF?!
HA, FINALLY!
WHAT WERE YOU DOING IN THERE?
QUICK! WE'VE GOT TO CLOSE THE PORTAL!
⁝HUMPH!⁝ I WISH PORTAL TRAVEL WASN'T SO RISKY! IT'S NOT NICE TO END UP STUCK BETWEEN TWO DIMENSIONS!
UHM... NO!

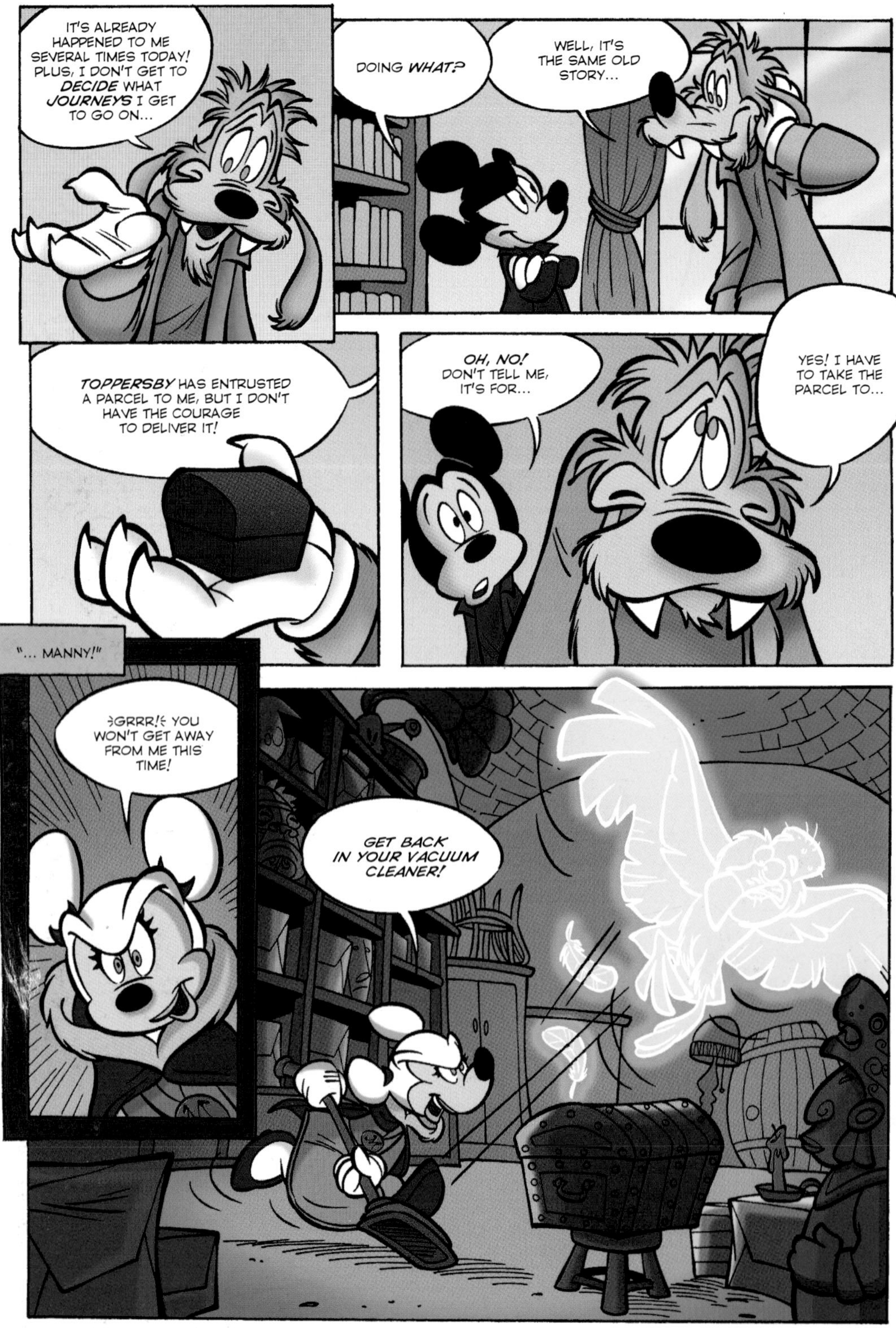
IT'S ALREADY HAPPENED TO ME SEVERAL TIMES TODAY! PLUS, I DON'T GET TO *DECIDE* WHAT *JOURNEYS* I GET TO GO ON...
DOING *WHAT?*
WELL, IT'S THE SAME OLD STORY...
TOPPERSBY HAS ENTRUSTED A PARCEL TO ME, BUT I DON'T HAVE THE COURAGE TO DELIVER IT!
OH, NO! DON'T TELL ME, IT'S FOR...
YES! I HAVE TO TAKE THE PARCEL TO...
"... MANNY!"
GRRR! YOU WON'T GET AWAY FROM ME THIS TIME!
GET BACK IN YOUR VACUUM CLEANER!

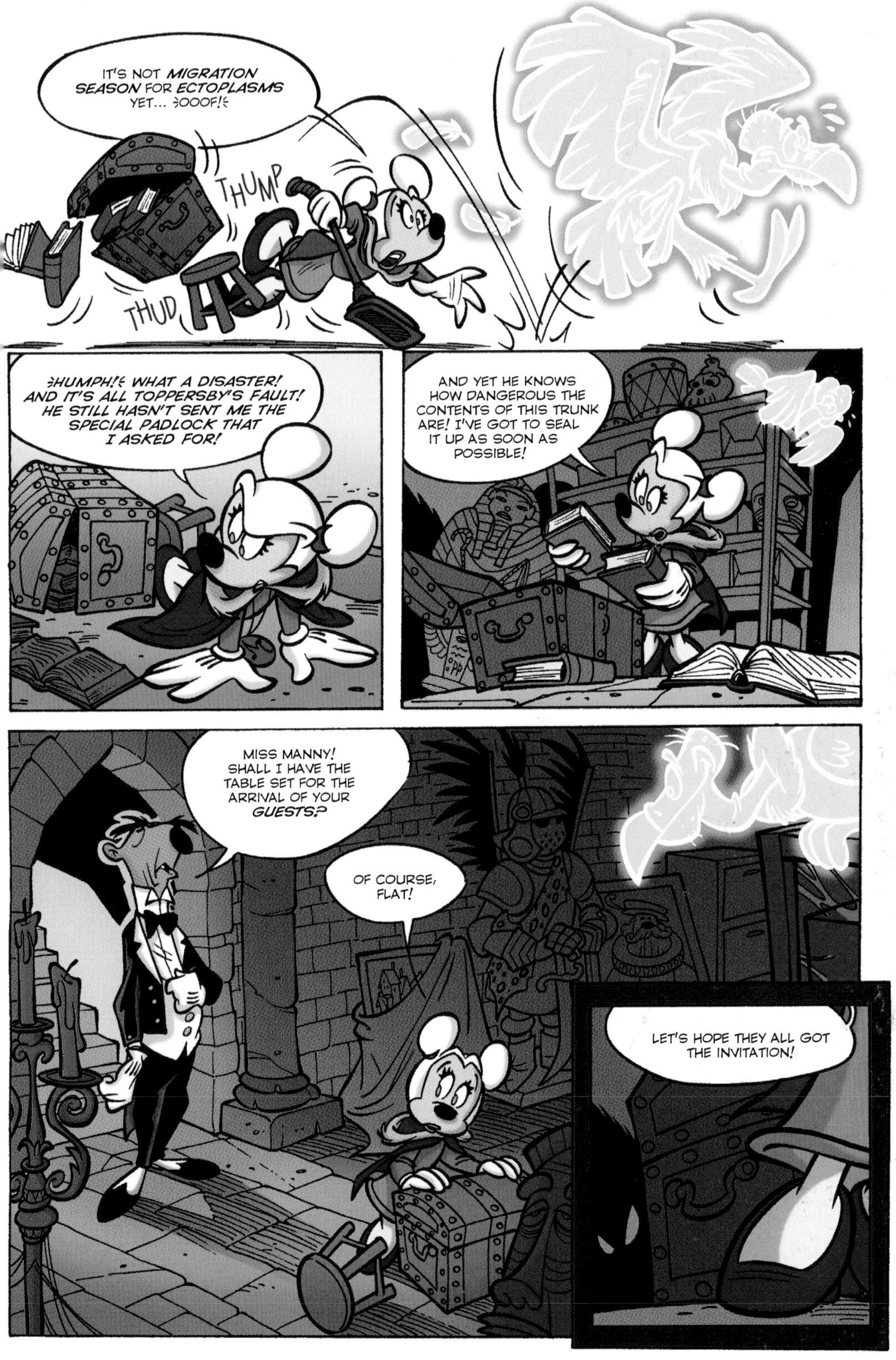
IT'S NOT MIGRATION SEASON FOR ECTOPLASMS YET... OOOF!
THUMP
THUD
HUMPH! WHAT A DISASTER! AND IT'S ALL TOPPERSBY'S FAULT! HE STILL HASN'T SENT ME THE SPECIAL PADLOCK THAT I ASKED FOR!
AND YET HE KNOWS HOW DANGEROUS THE CONTENTS OF THIS TRUNK ARE! I'VE GOT TO SEAL IT UP AS SOON AS POSSIBLE!
MISS MANNY! SHALL I HAVE THE TABLE SET FOR THE ARRIVAL OF YOUR GUESTS?
OF COURSE, FLAT!
LET'S HOPE THEY ALL GOT THE INVITATION!

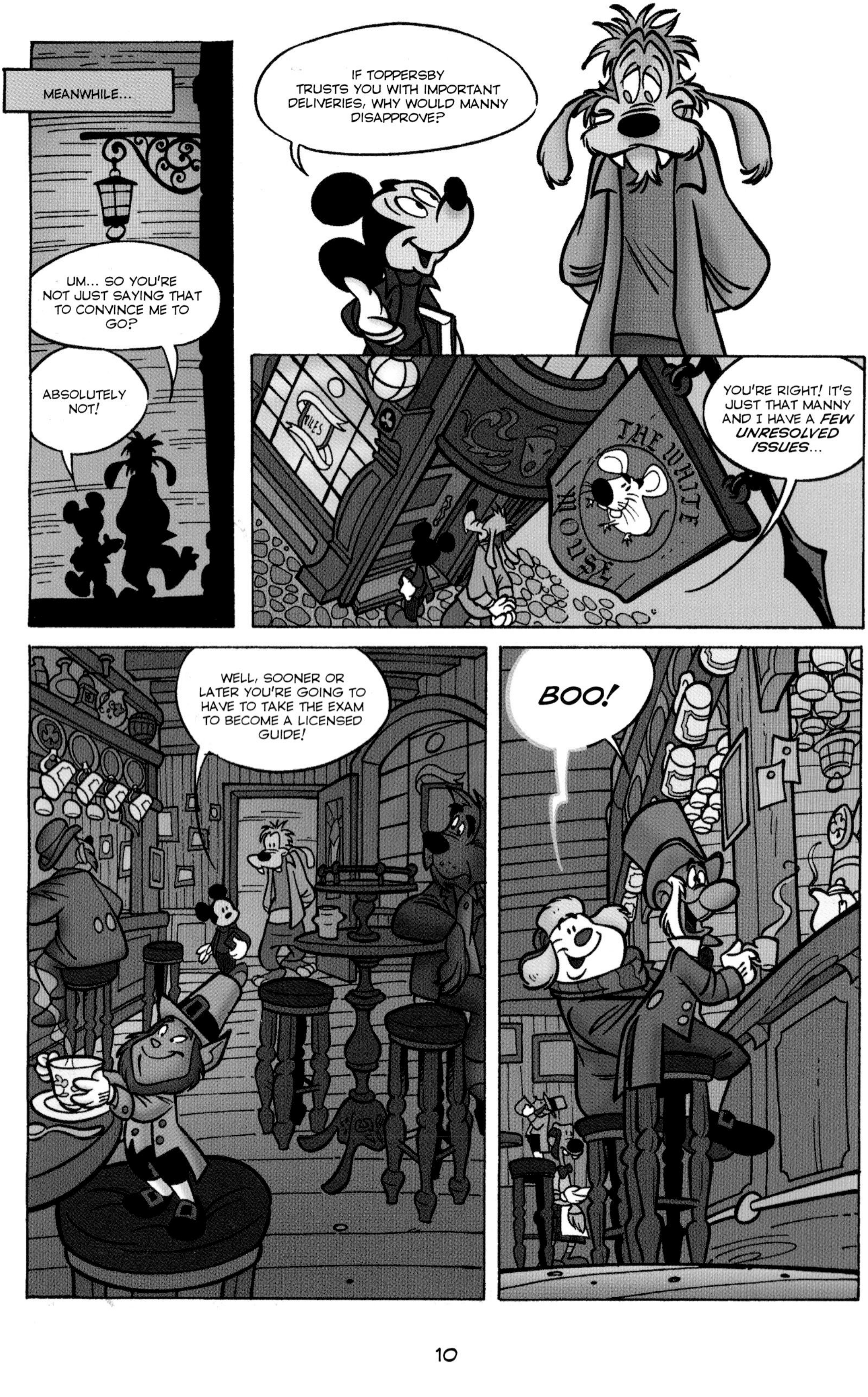
MEANWHILE...
IF TOPPERSBY TRUSTS YOU WITH IMPORTANT DELIVERIES, WHY WOULD MANNY DISAPPROVE?
UM... SO YOU'RE NOT JUST SAYING THAT TO CONVINCE ME TO GO?
ABSOLUTELY NOT!
THE WHITE MOUSE
YOU'RE RIGHT! IT'S JUST THAT MANNY AND I HAVE A *FEW UNRESOLVED ISSUES*...
WELL, SOONER OR LATER YOU'RE GOING TO HAVE TO TAKE THE EXAM TO BECOME A LICENSED GUIDE!
BOO!

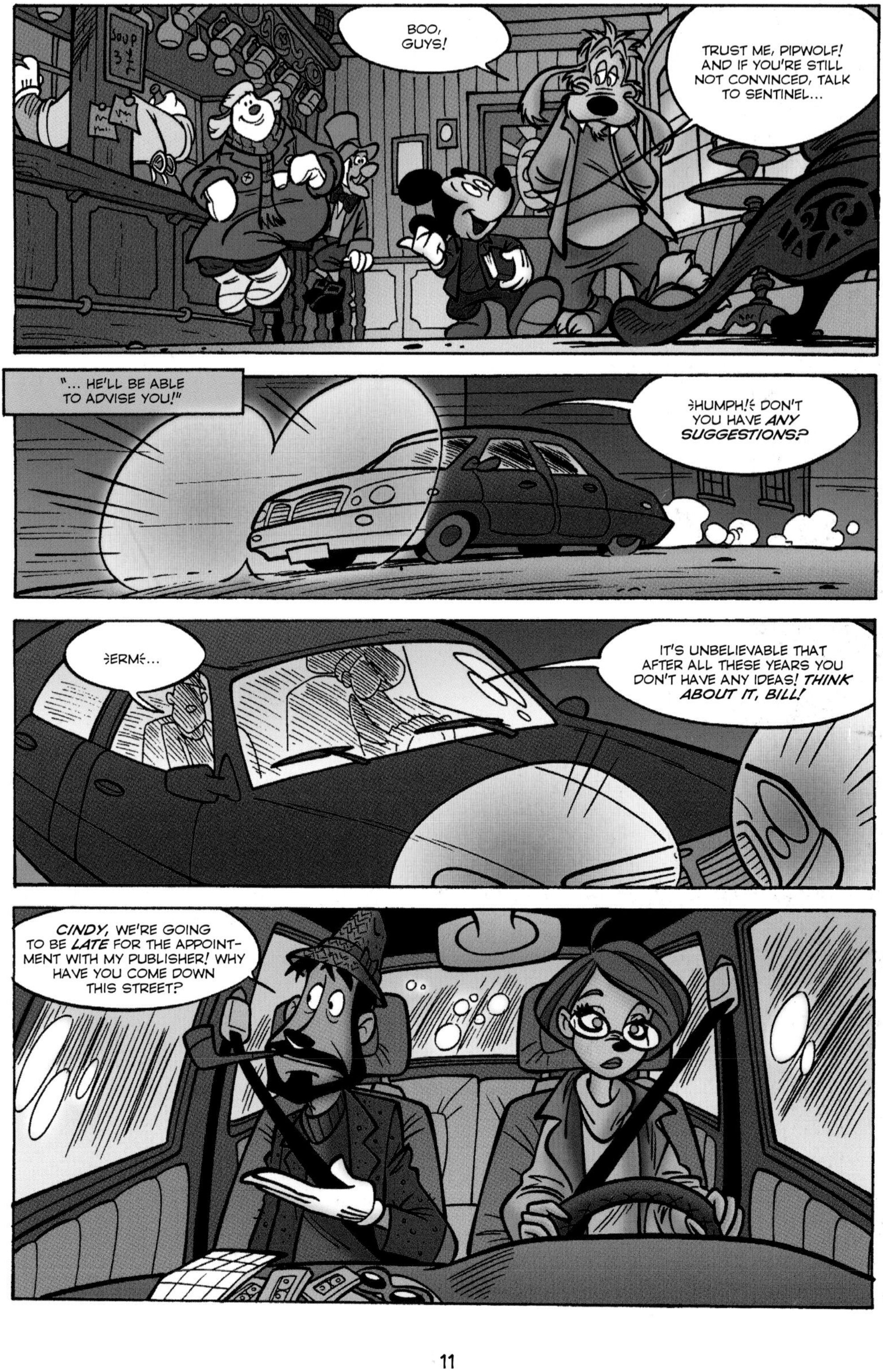
BOO, GUYS!
TRUST ME, PIPWOLF! AND IF YOU'RE STILL NOT CONVINCED, TALK TO SENTINEL...
SOUP
"... HE'LL BE ABLE TO ADVISE YOU!"
HUMPH! DON'T YOU HAVE *ANY SUGGESTIONS?*
ERM...
IT'S UNBELIEVABLE THAT AFTER ALL THESE YEARS YOU DON'T HAVE ANY IDEAS! *THINK ABOUT IT, BILL!*
CINDY, WE'RE GOING TO BE *LATE* FOR THE APPOINTMENT WITH MY PUBLISHER! WHY HAVE YOU COME DOWN THIS STREET?

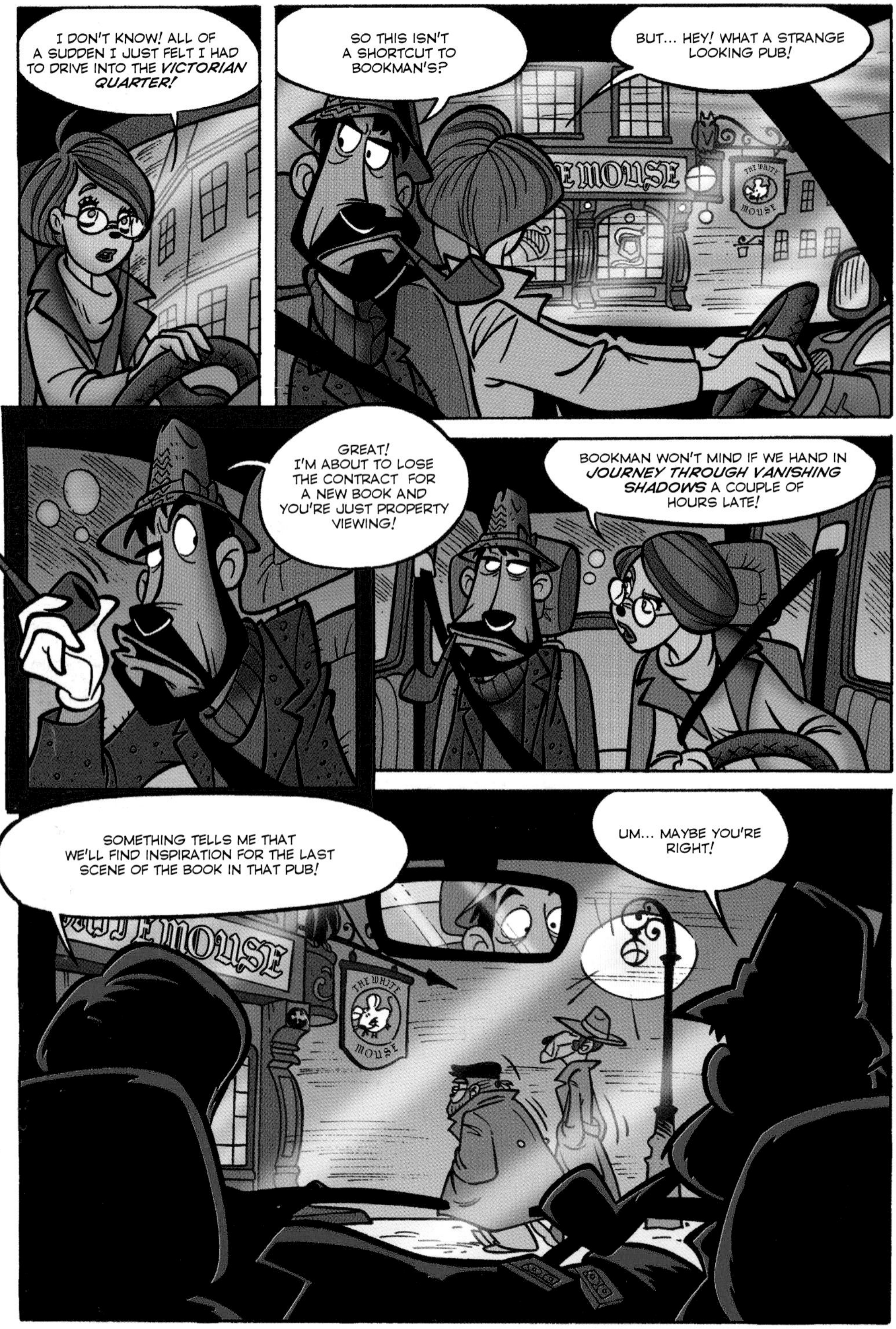
I DON'T KNOW! ALL OF A SUDDEN I JUST FELT I HAD TO DRIVE INTO THE *VICTORIAN QUARTER!*
SO THIS ISN'T A SHORTCUT TO BOOKMAN'S?
BUT... HEY! WHAT A STRANGE LOOKING PUB!
THE WHITE MOUSE
GREAT! I'M ABOUT TO LOSE THE CONTRACT FOR A NEW BOOK AND YOU'RE JUST PROPERTY VIEWING!
BOOKMAN WON'T MIND IF WE HAND IN ***JOURNEY THROUGH VANISHING SHADOWS*** A COUPLE OF HOURS LATE!
SOMETHING TELLS ME THAT WE'LL FIND INSPIRATION FOR THE LAST SCENE OF THE BOOK IN THAT PUB!
UM... MAYBE YOU'RE RIGHT!

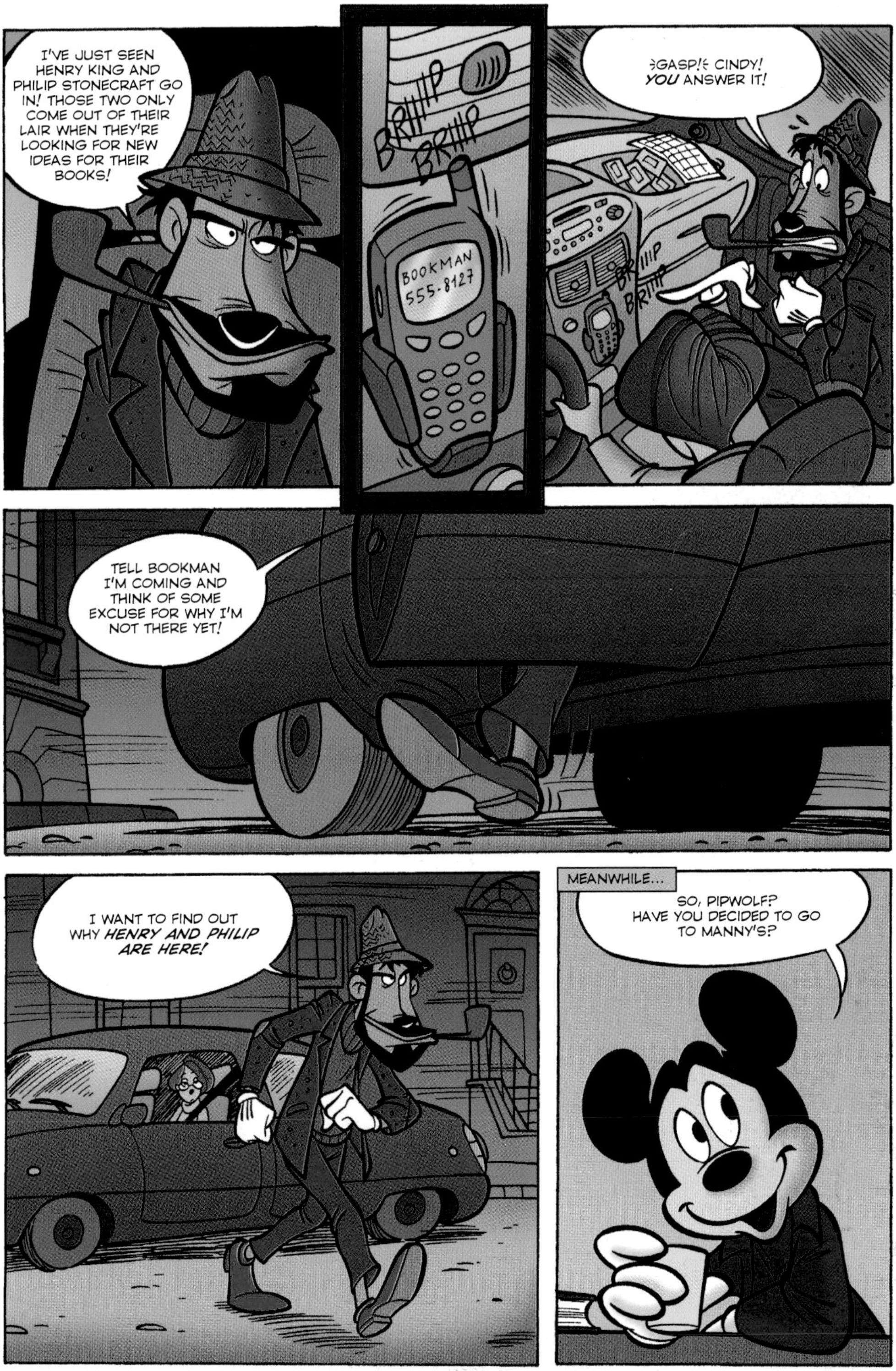
I'VE JUST SEEN HENRY KING AND PHILIP STONECRAFT GO IN! THOSE TWO ONLY COME OUT OF THEIR LAIR WHEN THEY'RE LOOKING FOR NEW IDEAS FOR THEIR BOOKS!
BRIIIP BRIIIP
BOOKMAN 555-8127
GASP! CINDY! YOU ANSWER IT!
BRIIIP BRIIIP
TELL BOOKMAN I'M COMING AND THINK OF SOME EXCUSE FOR WHY I'M NOT THERE YET!
I WANT TO FIND OUT WHY HENRY AND PHILIP ARE HERE!
MEANWHILE...
SO, PIPWOLF? HAVE YOU DECIDED TO GO TO MANNY'S?

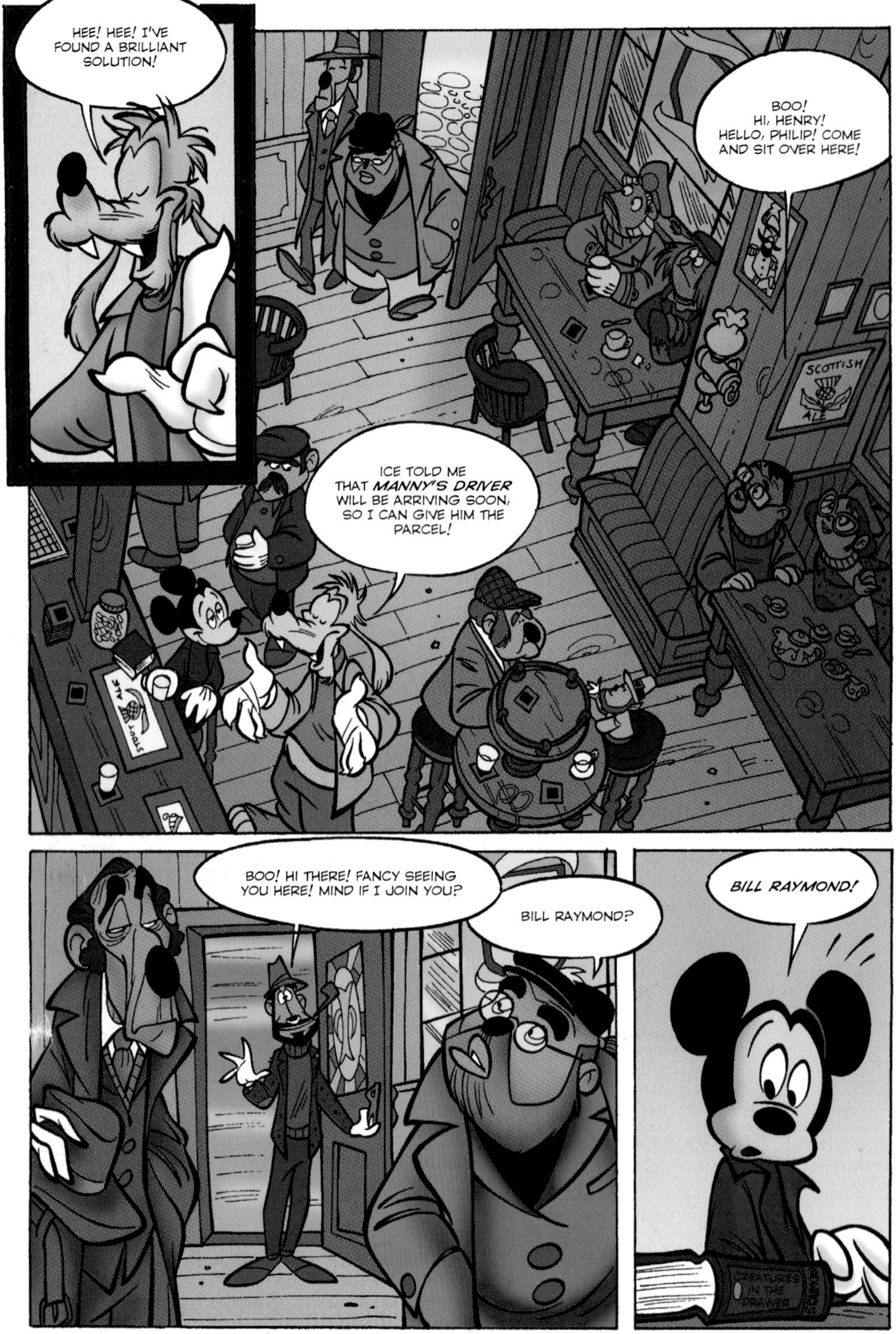
HEE! HEE! I'VE FOUND A BRILLIANT SOLUTION!
ICE TOLD ME THAT ***MANNY'S DRIVER*** WILL BE ARRIVING SOON, SO I CAN GIVE HIM THE PARCEL!
BOO! HI, HENRY! HELLO, PHILIP! COME AND SIT OVER HERE!
SCOTTISH ALE
BOO! HI THERE! FANCY SEEING YOU HERE! MIND IF I JOIN YOU?
BILL RAYMOND?
BILL RAYMOND!
CREATURES IN THE DRAWER

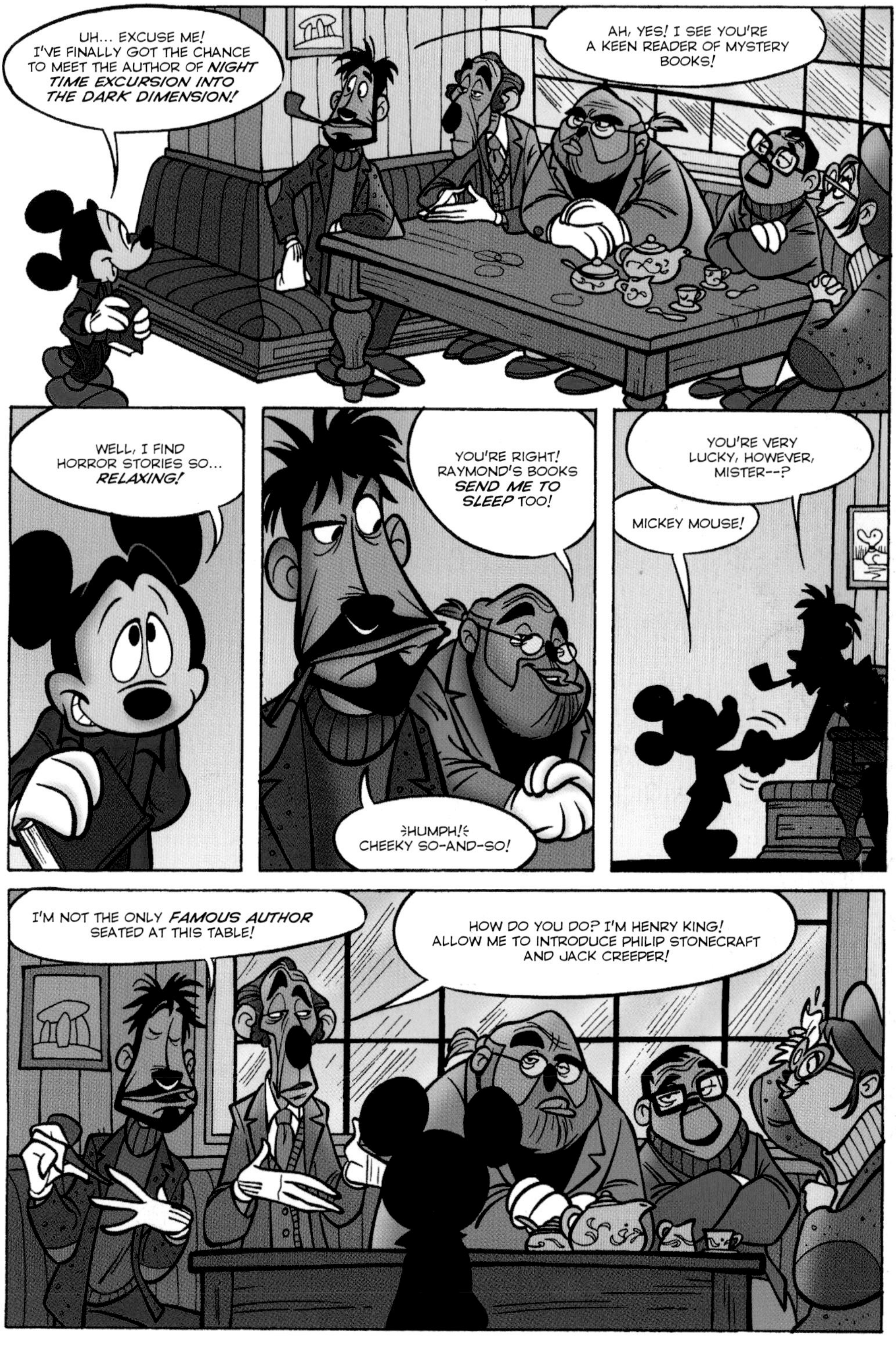
UH... EXCUSE ME! I'VE FINALLY GOT THE CHANCE TO MEET THE AUTHOR OF NIGHT TIME EXCURSION INTO THE DARK DIMENSION!
AH, YES! I SEE YOU'RE A KEEN READER OF MYSTERY BOOKS!
WELL, I FIND HORROR STORIES SO... RELAXING!
YOU'RE RIGHT! RAYMOND'S BOOKS SEND ME TO SLEEP TOO!
HUMPH! CHEEKY SO-AND-SO!
YOU'RE VERY LUCKY, HOWEVER, MISTER--?
MICKEY MOUSE!
I'M NOT THE ONLY FAMOUS AUTHOR SEATED AT THIS TABLE!
HOW DO YOU DO? I'M HENRY KING! ALLOW ME TO INTRODUCE PHILIP STONECRAFT AND JACK CREEPER!

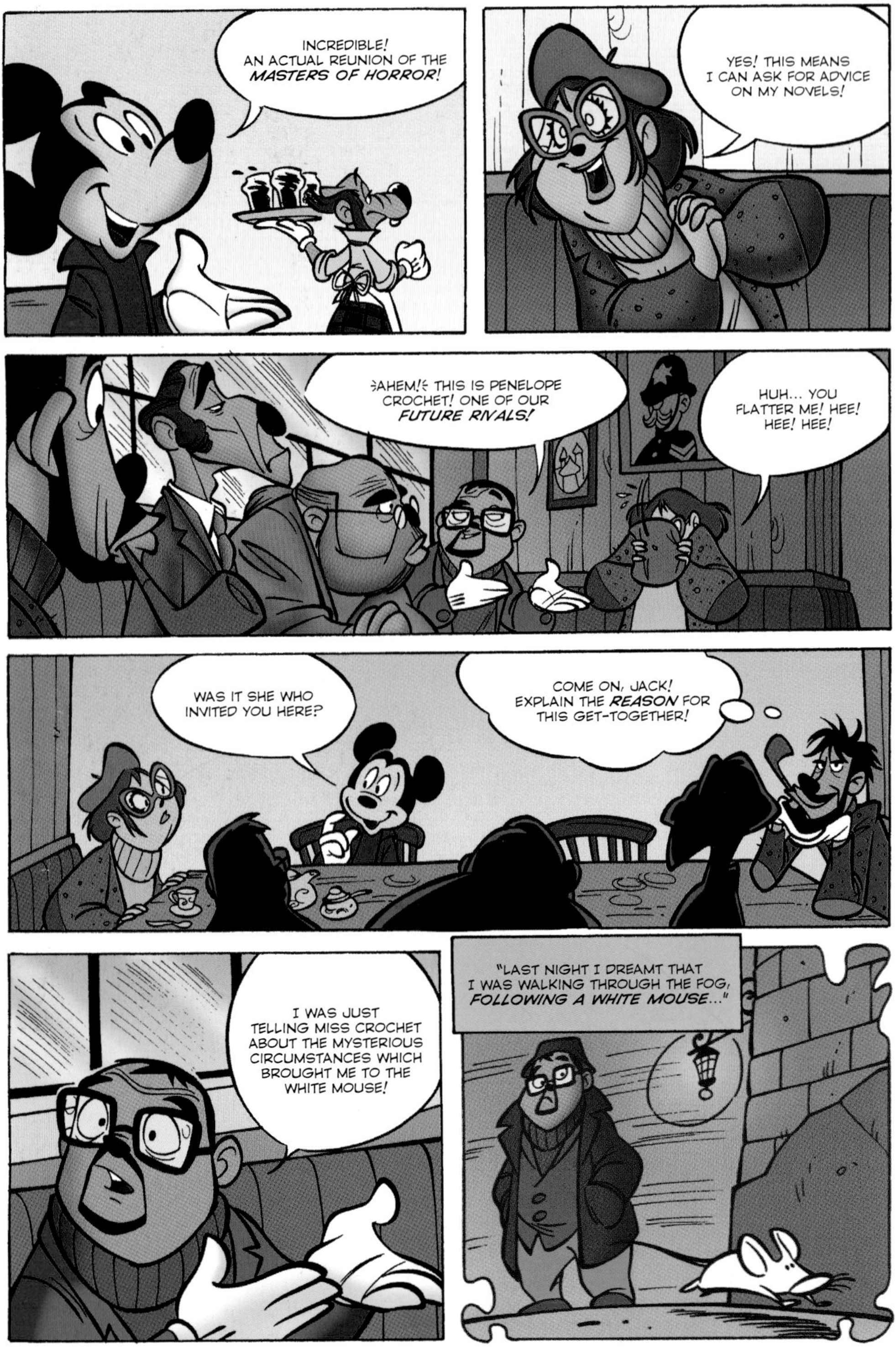
INCREDIBLE! AN ACTUAL REUNION OF THE MASTERS OF HORROR!
YES! THIS MEANS I CAN ASK FOR ADVICE ON MY NOVELS!
AHEM! THIS IS PENELOPE CROCHET! ONE OF OUR FUTURE RIVALS!
HUH... YOU FLATTER ME! HEE! HEE! HEE!
WAS IT SHE WHO INVITED YOU HERE?
COME ON, JACK! EXPLAIN THE REASON FOR THIS GET-TOGETHER!
I WAS JUST TELLING MISS CROCHET ABOUT THE MYSTERIOUS CIRCUMSTANCES WHICH BROUGHT ME TO THE WHITE MOUSE!
"LAST NIGHT I DREAMT THAT I WAS WALKING THROUGH THE FOG, FOLLOWING A WHITE MOUSE..."

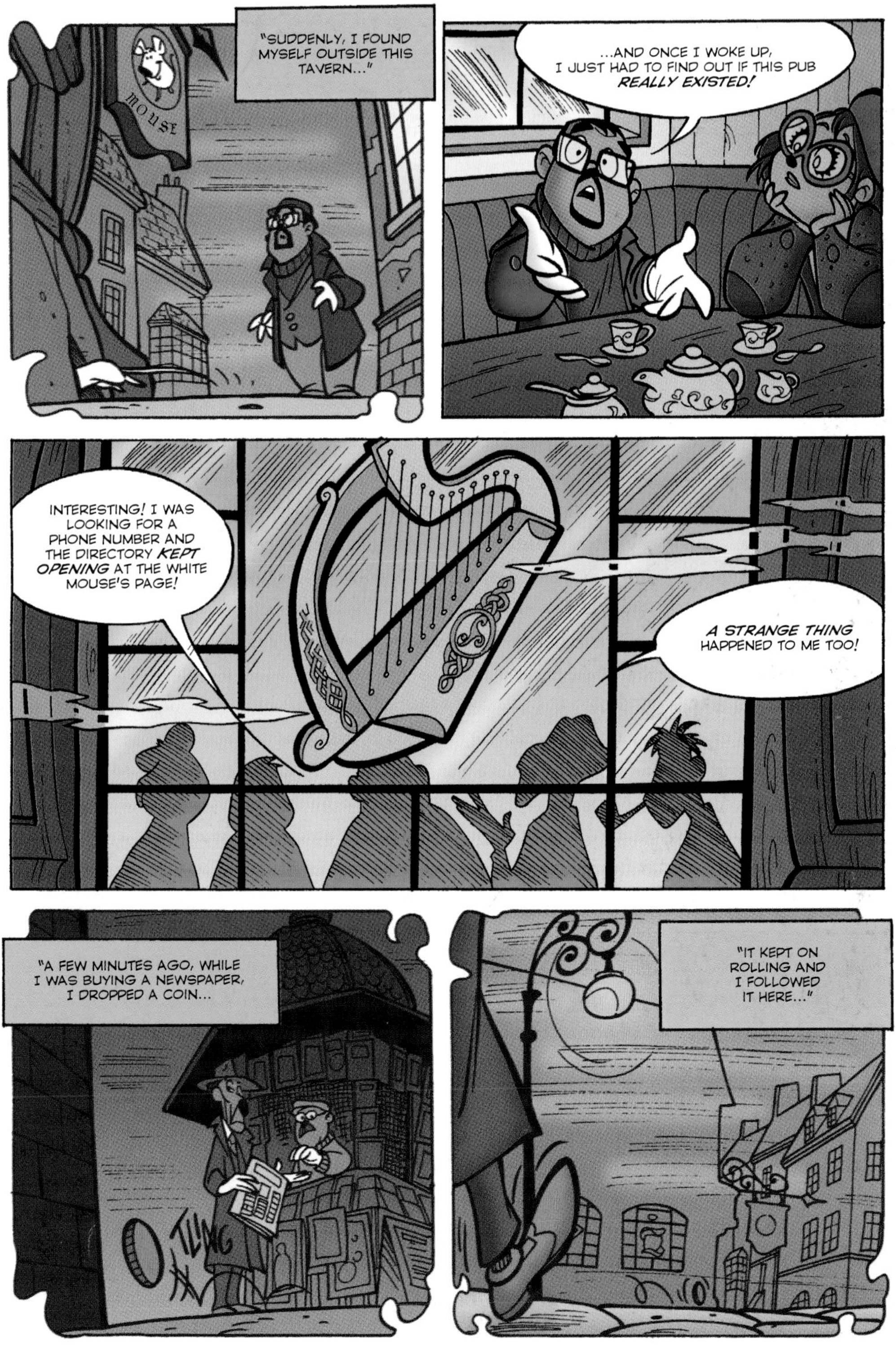
"SUDDENLY, I FOUND MYSELF OUTSIDE THIS TAVERN..."
MOUSE
...AND ONCE I WOKE UP, I JUST HAD TO FIND OUT IF THIS PUB *REALLY EXISTED!*
INTERESTING! I WAS LOOKING FOR A PHONE NUMBER AND THE DIRECTORY *KEPT OPENING* AT THE WHITE MOUSE'S PAGE!
A STRANGE THING HAPPENED TO ME TOO!
"A FEW MINUTES AGO, WHILE I WAS BUYING A NEWSPAPER, I DROPPED A COIN...
TLING
"IT KEPT ON ROLLING AND I FOLLOWED IT HERE..."

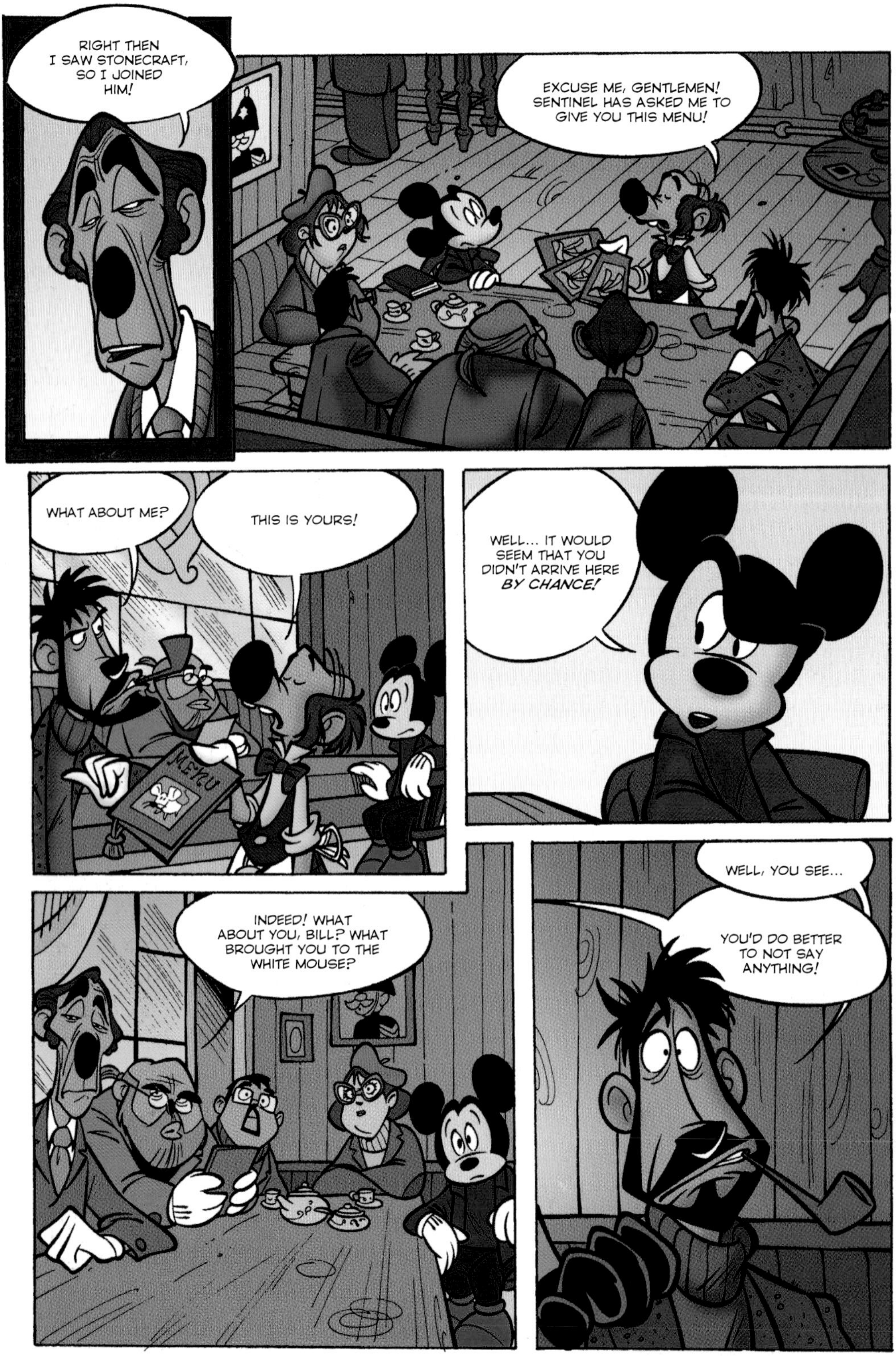
RIGHT THEN I SAW STONECRAFT, SO I JOINED HIM!
EXCUSE ME, GENTLEMEN! SENTINEL HAS ASKED ME TO GIVE YOU THIS MENU!
WHAT ABOUT ME?
THIS IS YOURS!
MENU
WELL... IT WOULD SEEM THAT YOU DIDN'T ARRIVE HERE *BY CHANCE!*
INDEED! WHAT ABOUT YOU, BILL? WHAT BROUGHT YOU TO THE WHITE MOUSE?
WELL, YOU SEE...
YOU'D DO BETTER TO NOT SAY ANYTHING!

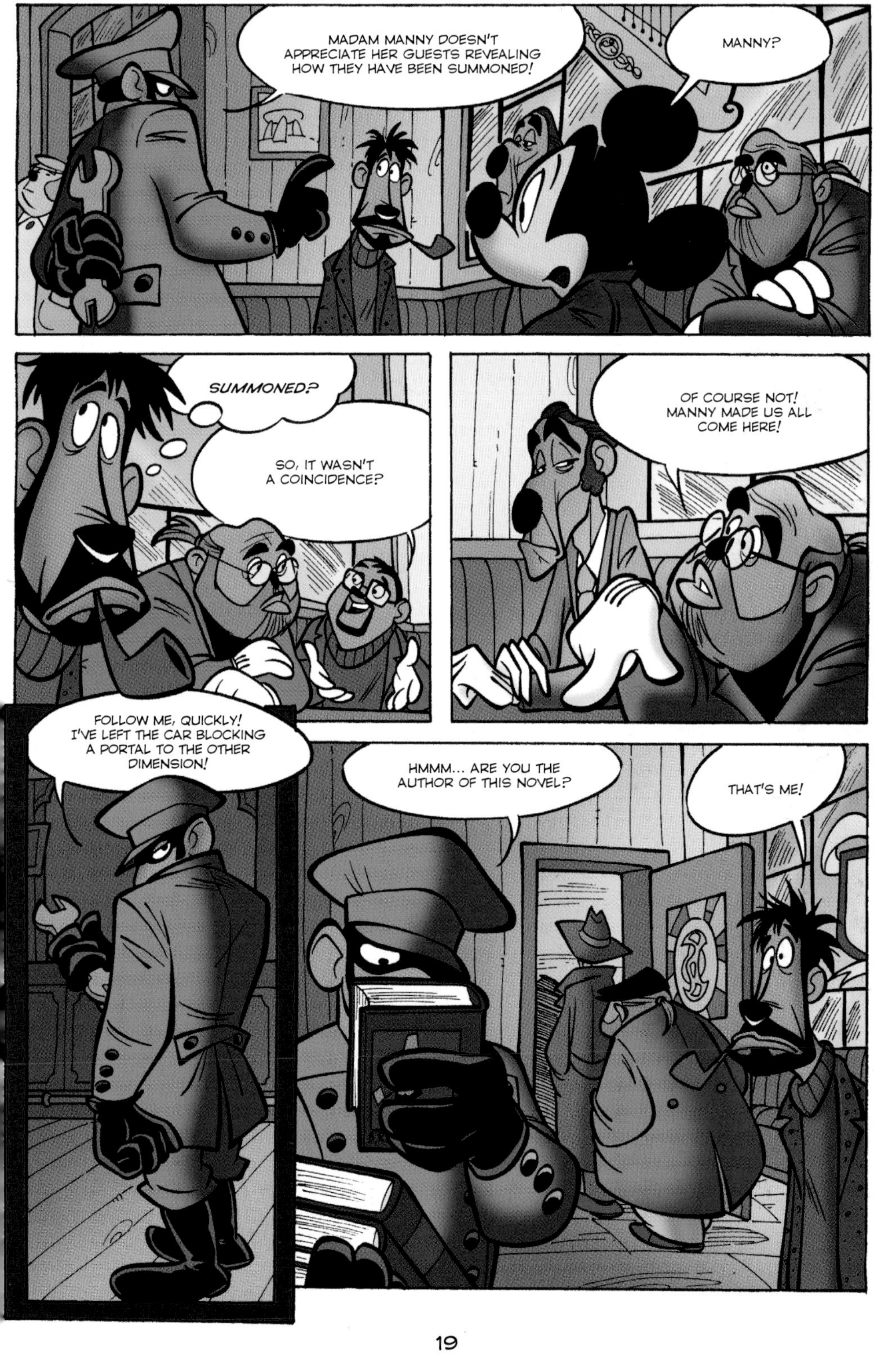
MADAM MANNY DOESN'T APPRECIATE HER GUESTS REVEALING HOW THEY HAVE BEEN SUMMONED!
MANNY?
SUMMONED?
SO, IT WASN'T A COINCIDENCE?
OF COURSE NOT! MANNY MADE US ALL COME HERE!
FOLLOW ME, QUICKLY! I'VE LEFT THE CAR BLOCKING A PORTAL TO THE OTHER DIMENSION!
HMMM... ARE YOU THE AUTHOR OF THIS NOVEL?
THAT'S ME!

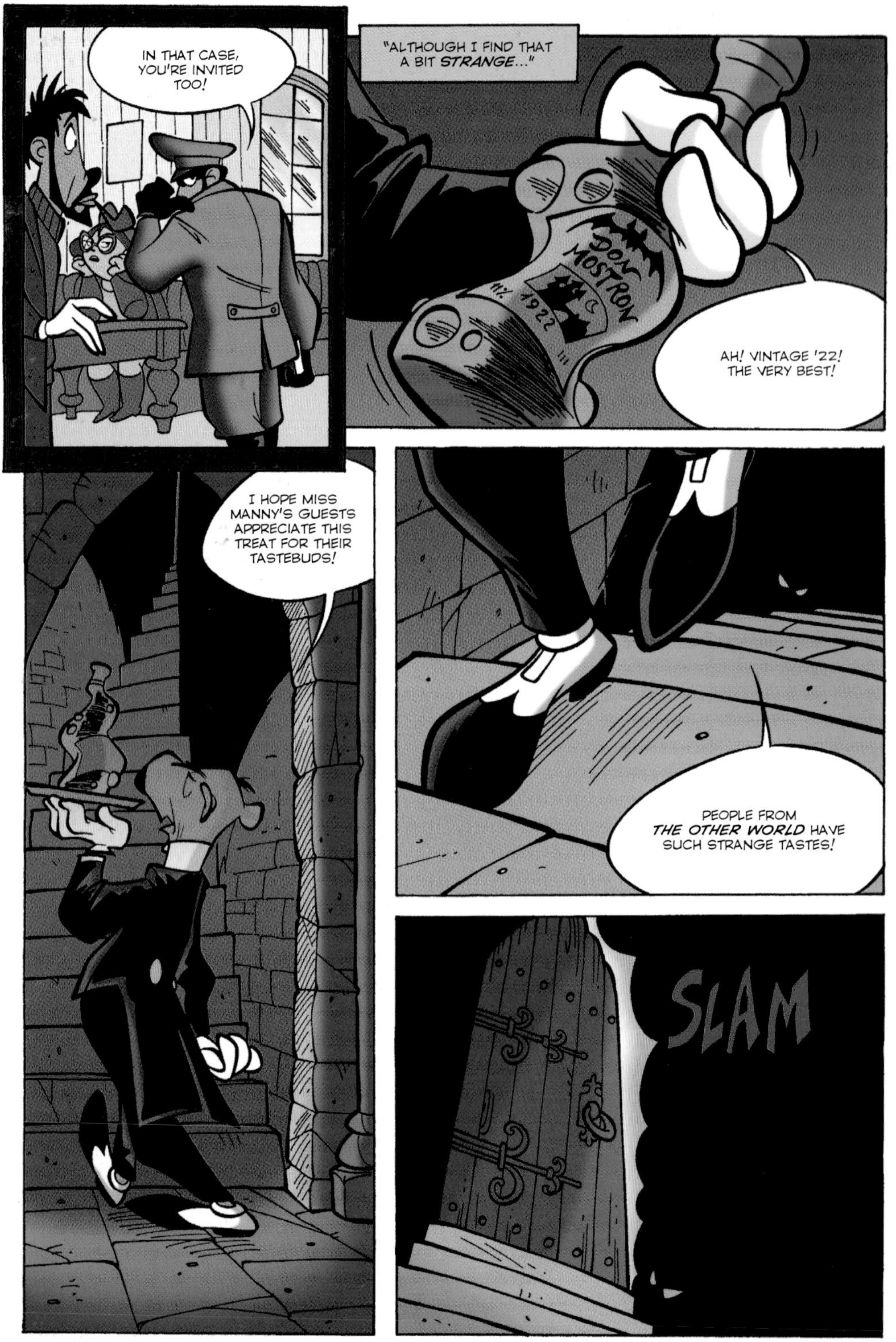

IN THAT CASE, YOU'RE INVITED TOO!
"ALTHOUGH I FIND THAT A BIT STRANGE..."
DON MOSTRON
1922
AH! VINTAGE '22! THE VERY BEST!
I HOPE MISS MANNY'S GUESTS APPRECIATE THIS TREAT FOR THEIR TASTEBUDS!
PEOPLE FROM THE OTHER WORLD HAVE SUCH STRANGE TASTES!
SLAM

GEE... I'VE ACCEPTED THE INVITATION, BUT... WHO IS THIS MANNY?

SO YOU'VE NEVER BEEN TO HER LITERARY SALON, EH? YOU'RE GOING TO LOVE IT!

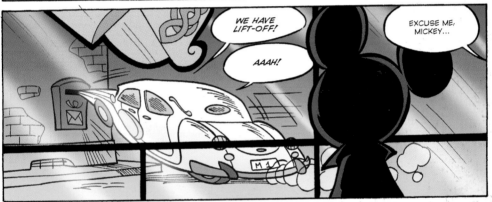

WE HAVE LIFT-OFF!

AAAH!

EXCUSE ME, MICKEY...

HAVE YOU SEEN MANNY'S DRIVER? TWOSTEPS TELLS ME HE JUST CAME IN!

ACTUALLY, HE JUST LEFT NOW!

OH, NO!

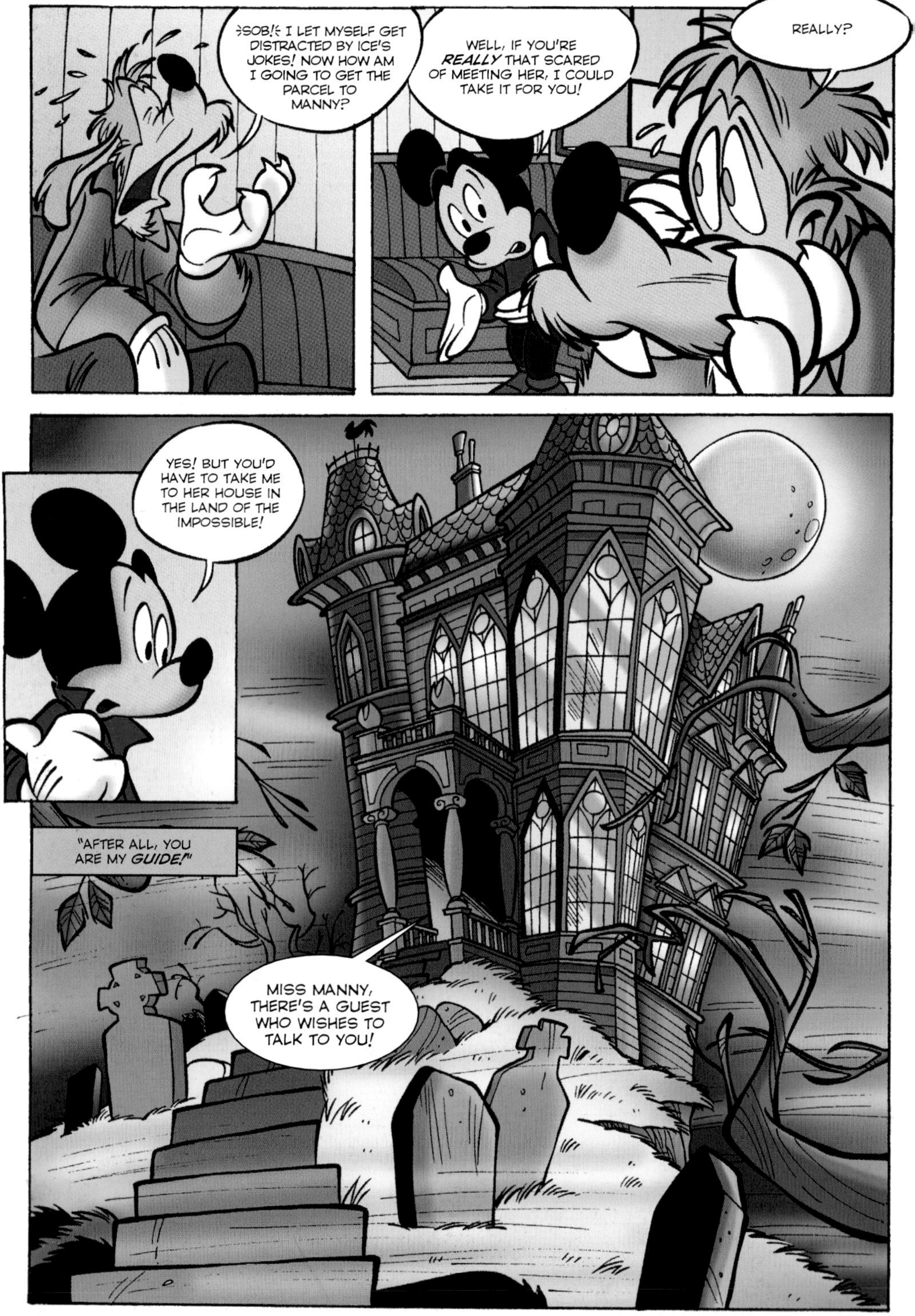

SOB! I LET MYSELF GET DISTRACTED BY ICE'S JOKES! NOW HOW AM I GOING TO GET THE PARCEL TO MANNY?
WELL, IF YOU'RE REALLY THAT SCARED OF MEETING HER, I COULD TAKE IT FOR YOU!
REALLY?
YES! BUT YOU'D HAVE TO TAKE ME TO HER HOUSE IN THE LAND OF THE IMPOSSIBLE!
"AFTER ALL, YOU ARE MY GUIDE!"
MISS MANNY, THERE'S A GUEST WHO WISHES TO TALK TO YOU!

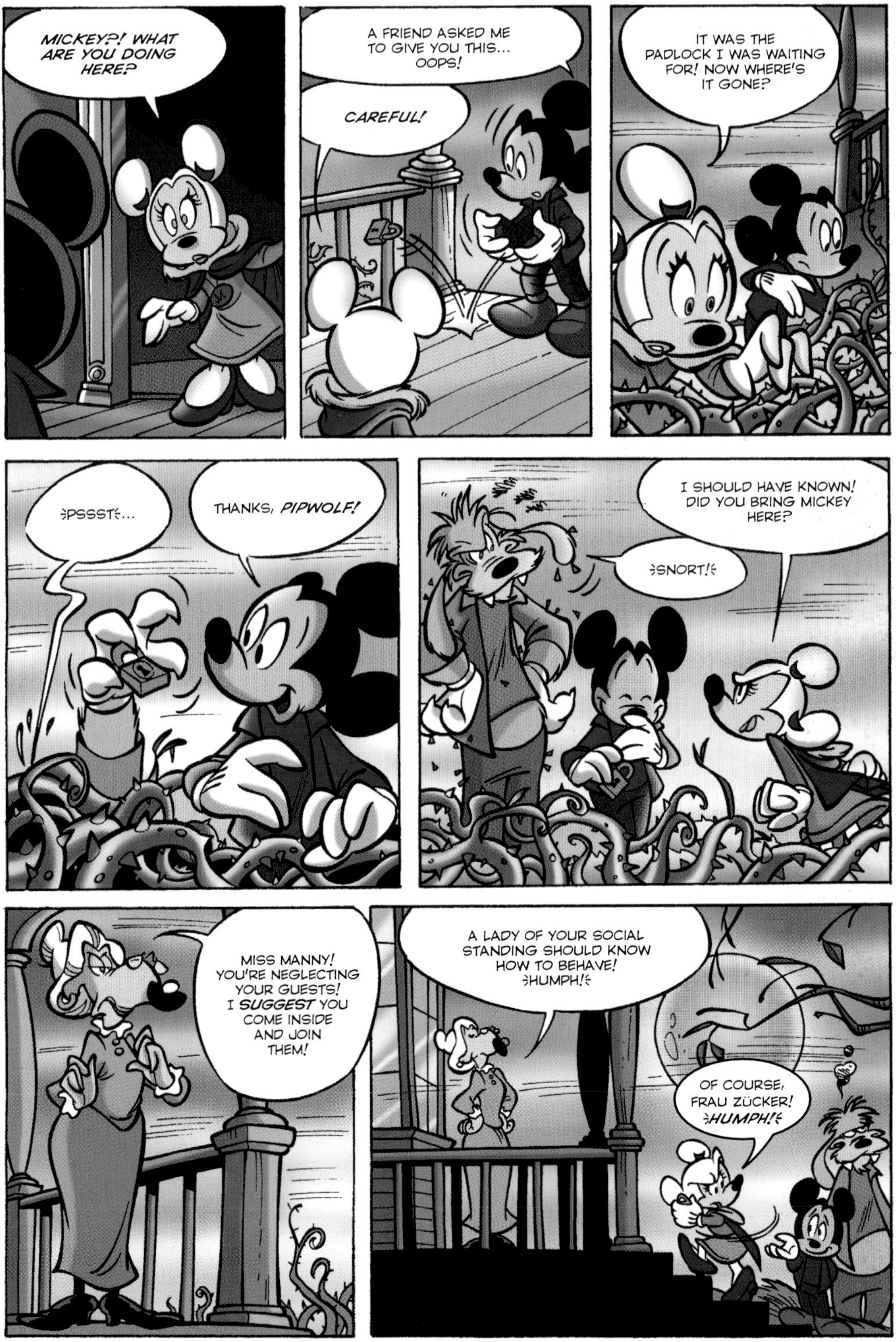
MICKEY?! WHAT ARE YOU DOING HERE?
A FRIEND ASKED ME TO GIVE YOU THIS... OOPS!
CAREFUL!
IT WAS THE PADLOCK I WAS WAITING FOR! NOW WHERE'S IT GONE?
PSSST...
THANKS, PIPWOLF!
I SHOULD HAVE KNOWN! DID YOU BRING MICKEY HERE?
SNORT!
MISS MANNY! YOU'RE NEGLECTING YOUR GUESTS! I SUGGEST YOU COME INSIDE AND JOIN THEM!
A LADY OF YOUR SOCIAL STANDING SHOULD KNOW HOW TO BEHAVE! HUMPH!
OF COURSE, FRAU ZÜCKER! HUMPH!

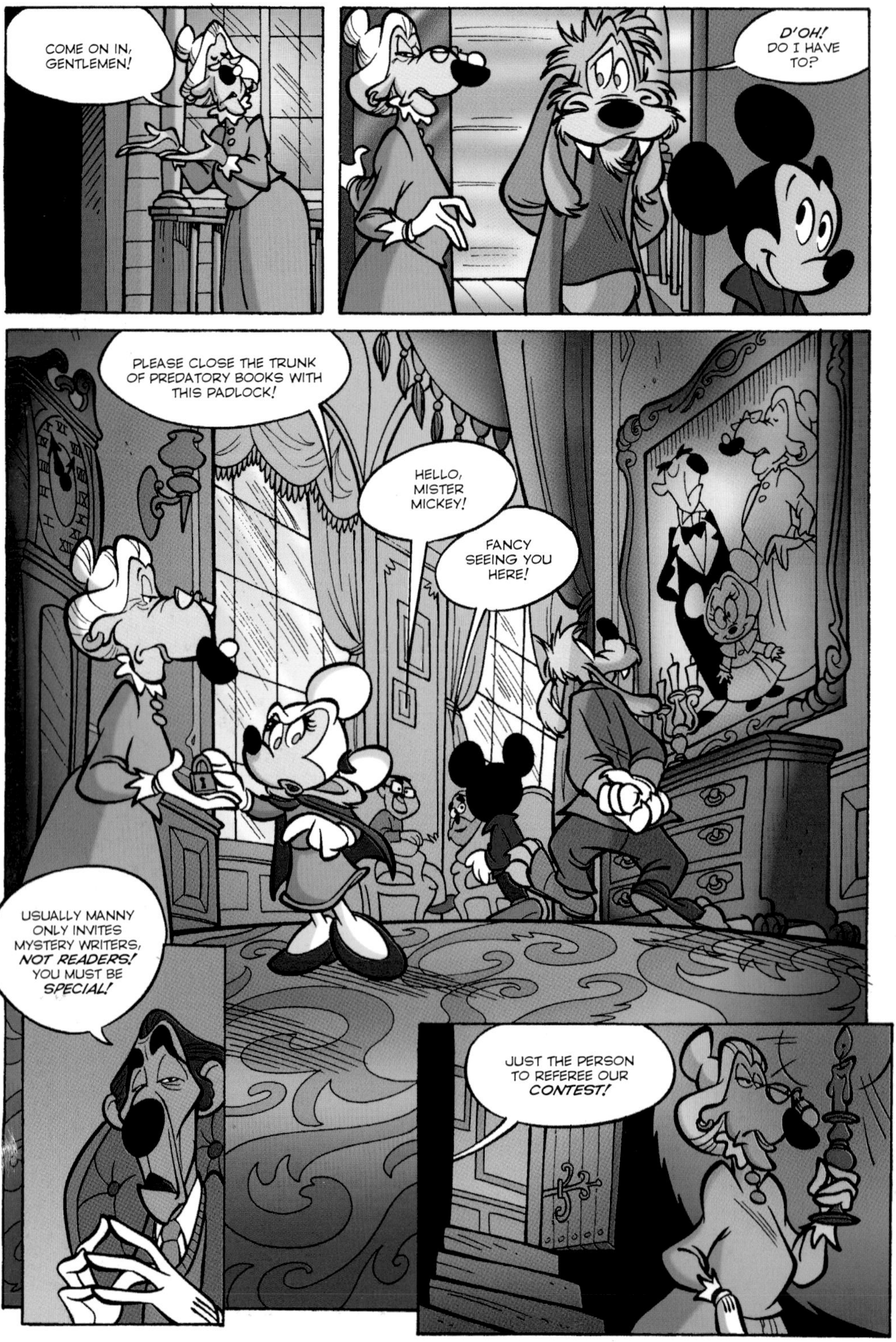
COME ON IN, GENTLEMEN!
D'OH! DO I HAVE TO?
PLEASE CLOSE THE TRUNK OF PREDATORY BOOKS WITH THIS PADLOCK!
HELLO, MISTER MICKEY!
FANCY SEEING YOU HERE!
USUALLY MANNY ONLY INVITES MYSTERY WRITERS, NOT READERS! YOU MUST BE SPECIAL!
JUST THE PERSON TO REFEREE OUR CONTEST!

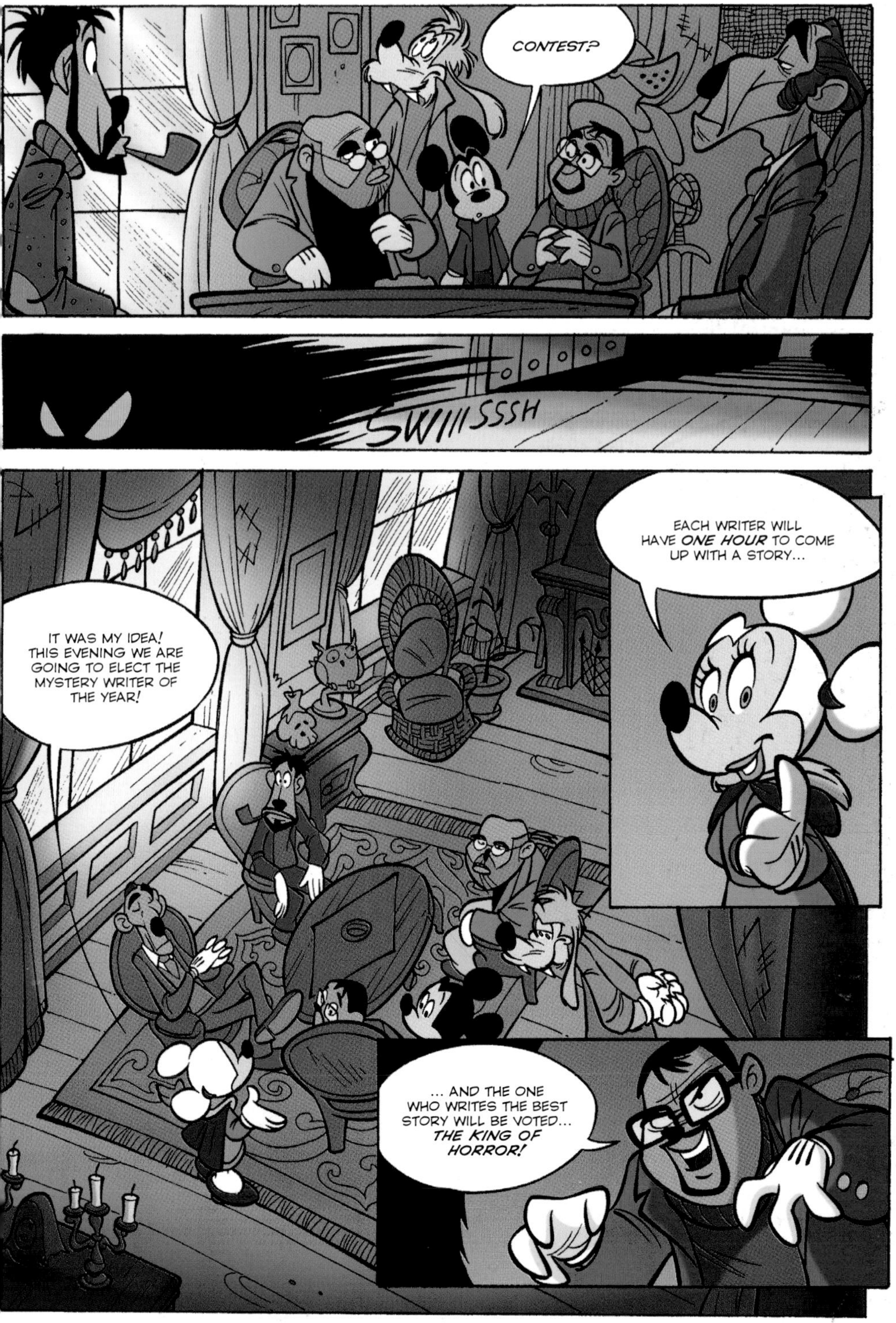

CONTEST?
SWIIISSSH
IT WAS MY IDEA! THIS EVENING WE ARE GOING TO ELECT THE MYSTERY WRITER OF THE YEAR!
EACH WRITER WILL HAVE *ONE HOUR* TO COME UP WITH A STORY...
... AND THE ONE WHO WRITES THE BEST STORY WILL BE VOTED... ***THE KING OF HORROR!***

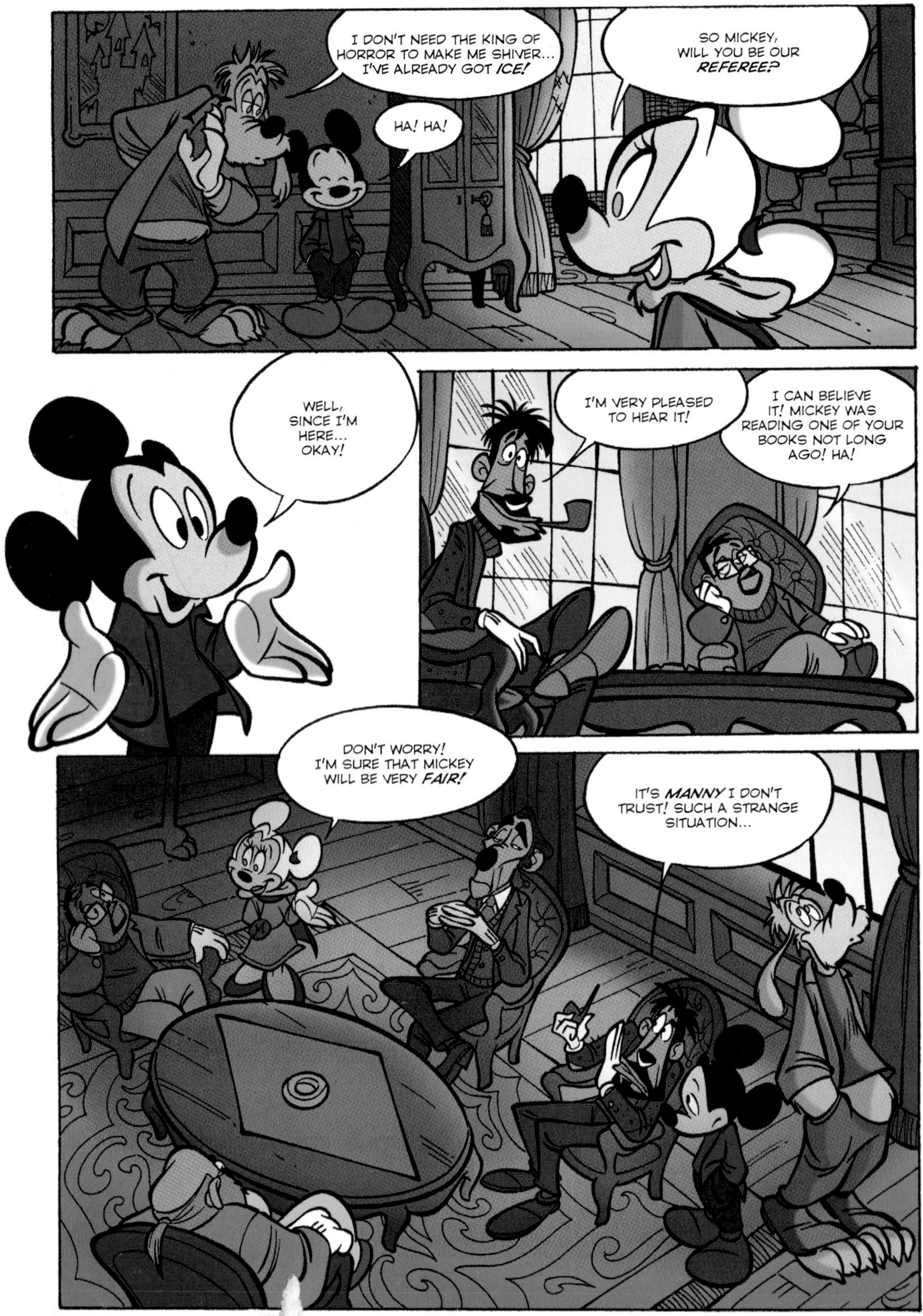
I DON'T NEED THE KING OF HORROR TO MAKE ME SHIVER... I'VE ALREADY GOT ICE!
HA! HA!
SO MICKEY, WILL YOU BE OUR REFEREE?
WELL, SINCE I'M HERE... OKAY!
I'M VERY PLEASED TO HEAR IT!
I CAN BELIEVE IT! MICKEY WAS READING ONE OF YOUR BOOKS NOT LONG AGO! HA!
DON'T WORRY! I'M SURE THAT MICKEY WILL BE VERY FAIR!
IT'S MANNY I DON'T TRUST! SUCH A STRANGE SITUATION...

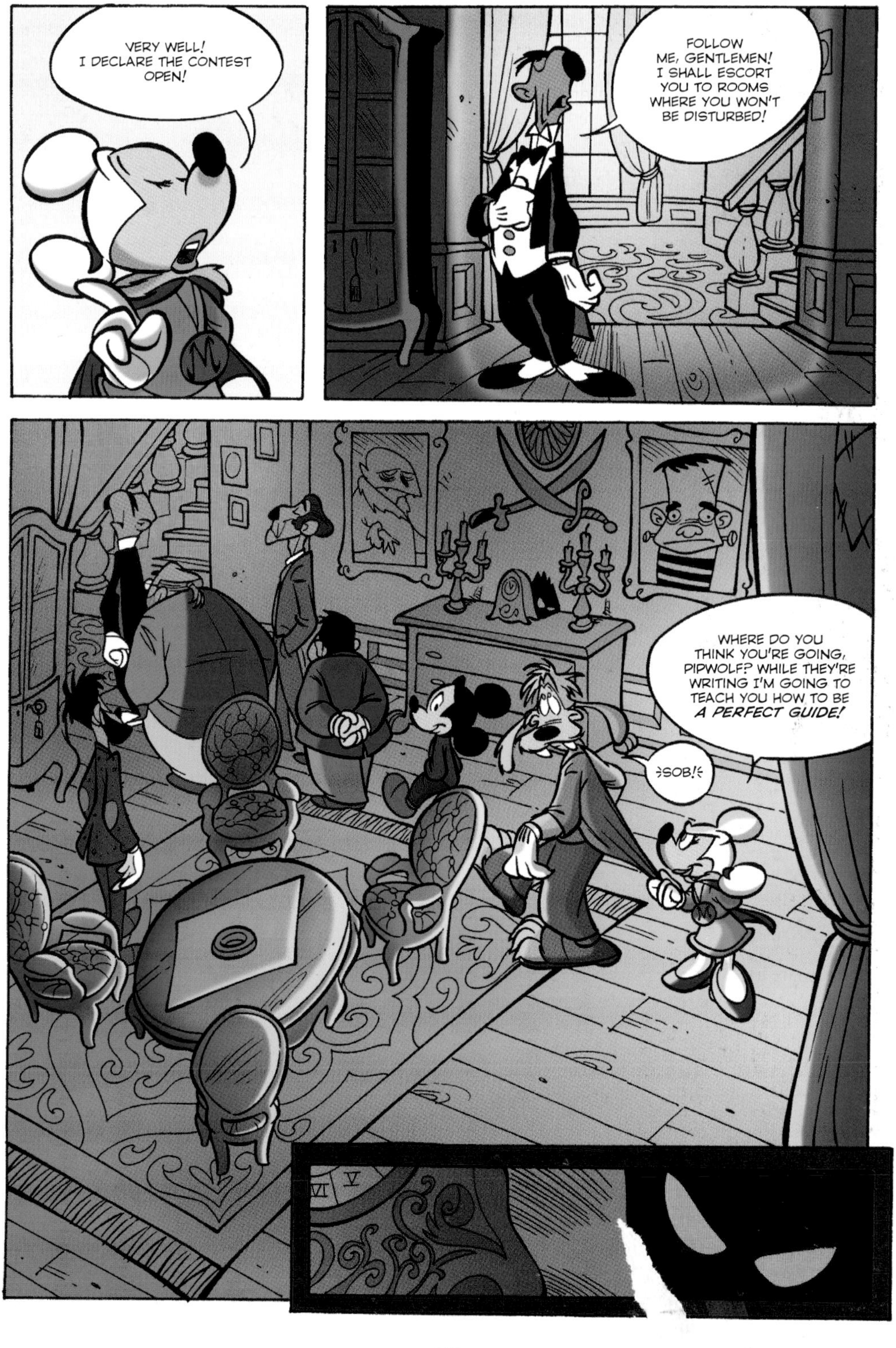
VERY WELL! I DECLARE THE CONTEST OPEN!
FOLLOW ME, GENTLEMEN! I SHALL ESCORT YOU TO ROOMS WHERE YOU WON'T BE DISTURBED!
WHERE DO YOU THINK YOU'RE GOING, PIPWOLF? WHILE THEY'RE WRITING I'M GOING TO TEACH YOU HOW TO BE *A PERFECT GUIDE!*
SOB!

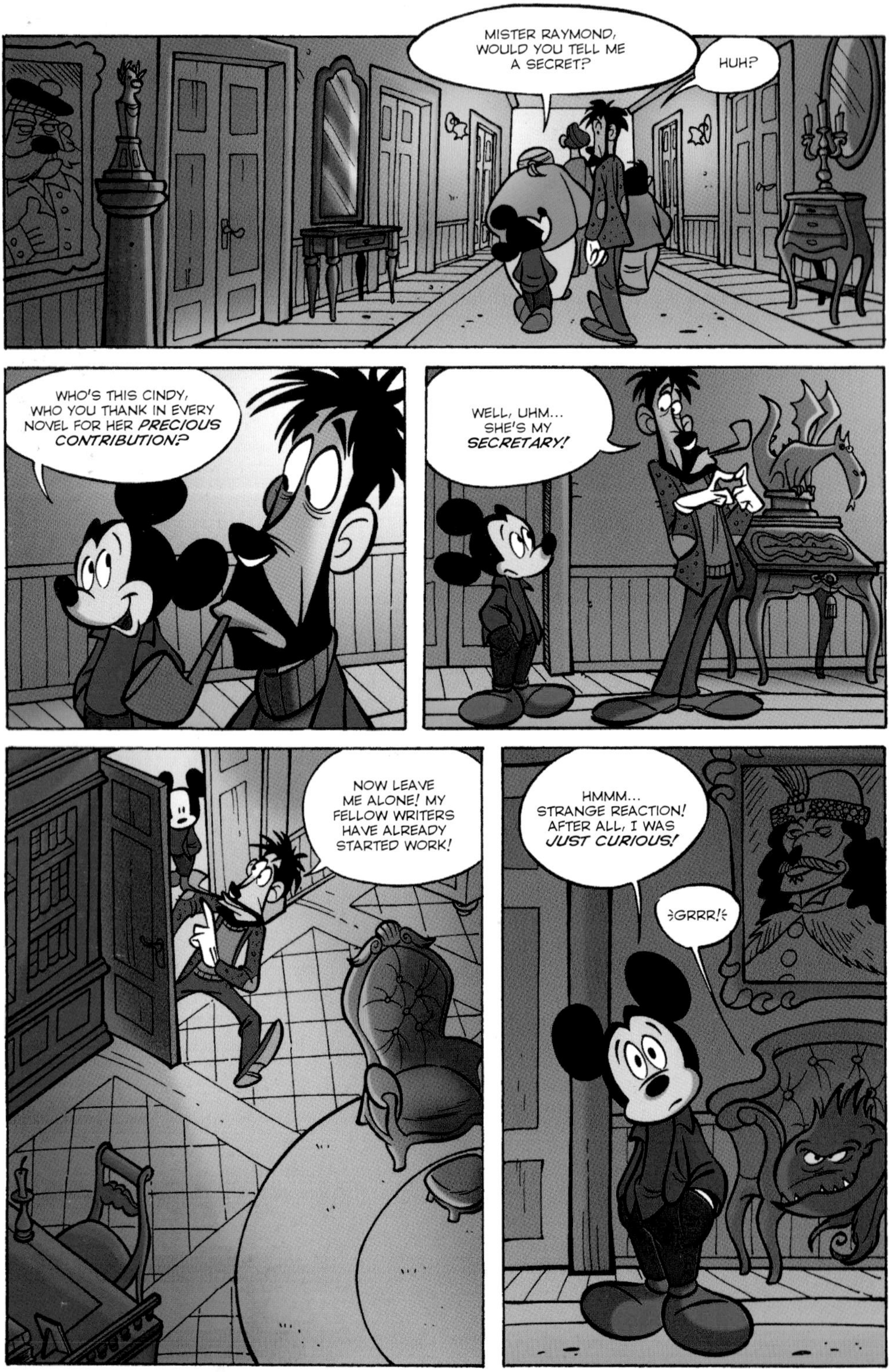
MISTER RAYMOND, WOULD YOU TELL ME A SECRET?
HUH?
WHO'S THIS CINDY, WHO YOU THANK IN EVERY NOVEL FOR HER PRECIOUS CONTRIBUTION?
WELL, UHM... SHE'S MY SECRETARY!
NOW LEAVE ME ALONE! MY FELLOW WRITERS HAVE ALREADY STARTED WORK!
HMMM... STRANGE REACTION! AFTER ALL, I WAS JUST CURIOUS!
GRRR!

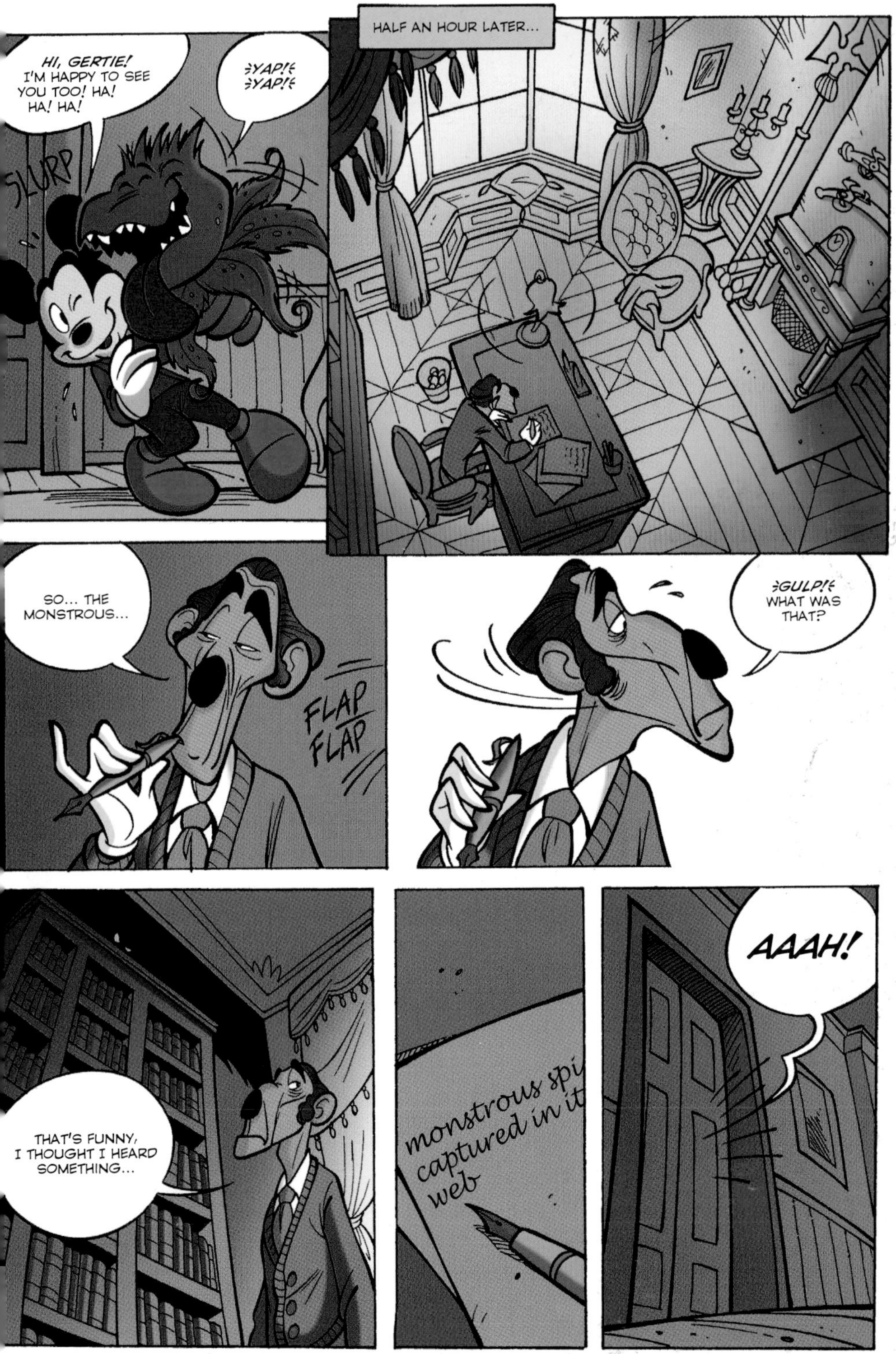
HI, GERTIE! I'M HAPPY TO SEE YOU TOO! HA! HA! HA!
SLURP
YAP! YAP!
HALF AN HOUR LATER...
SO... THE MONSTROUS...
FLAP FLAP
GULP! WHAT WAS THAT?
THAT'S FUNNY, I THOUGHT I HEARD SOMETHING...
monstrous spi
captured in it
web
AAAH!

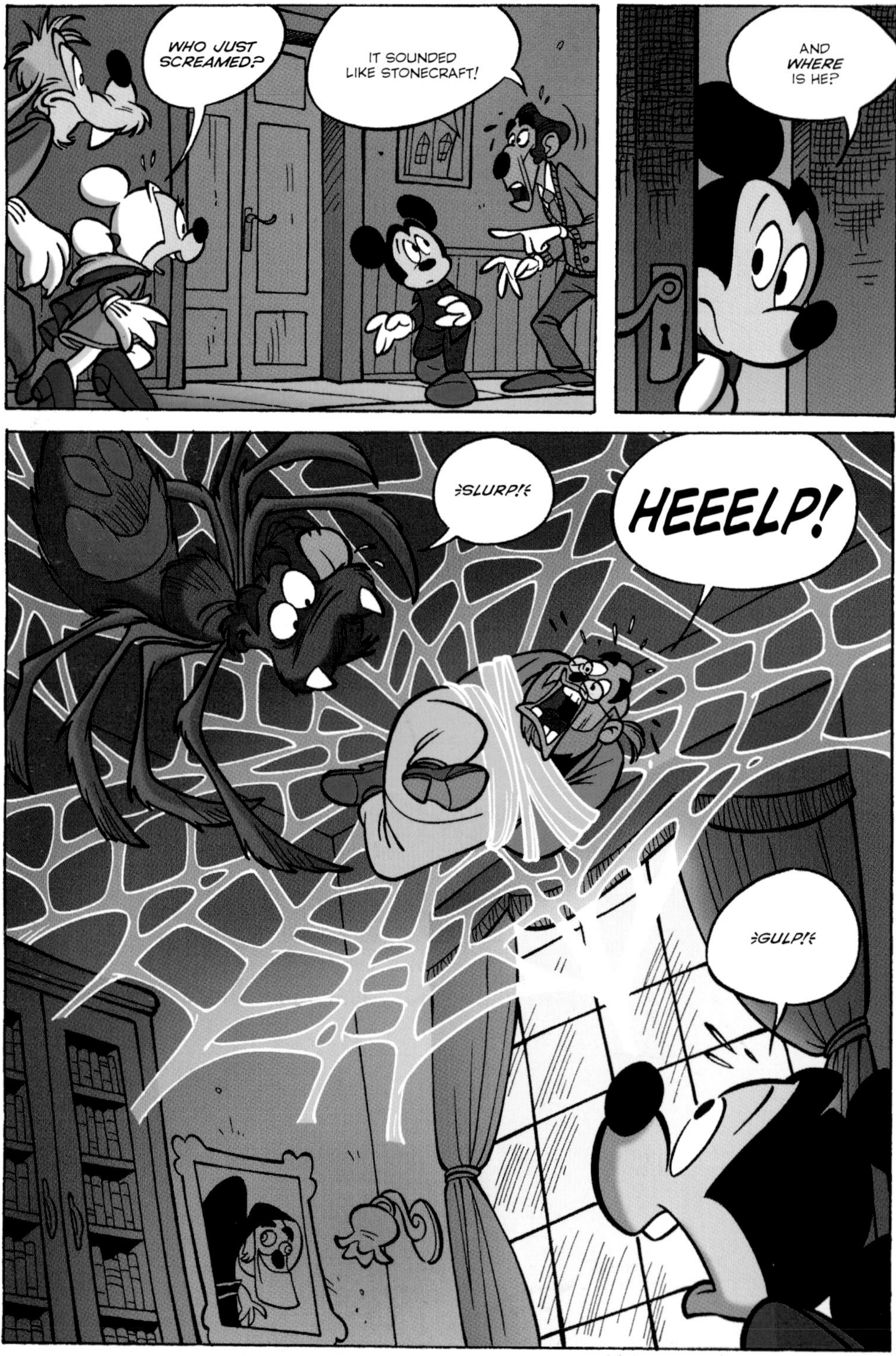
WHO JUST SCREAMED?
IT SOUNDED LIKE STONECRAFT!
AND WHERE IS HE?
SLURP!
HEEELP!
GULP!

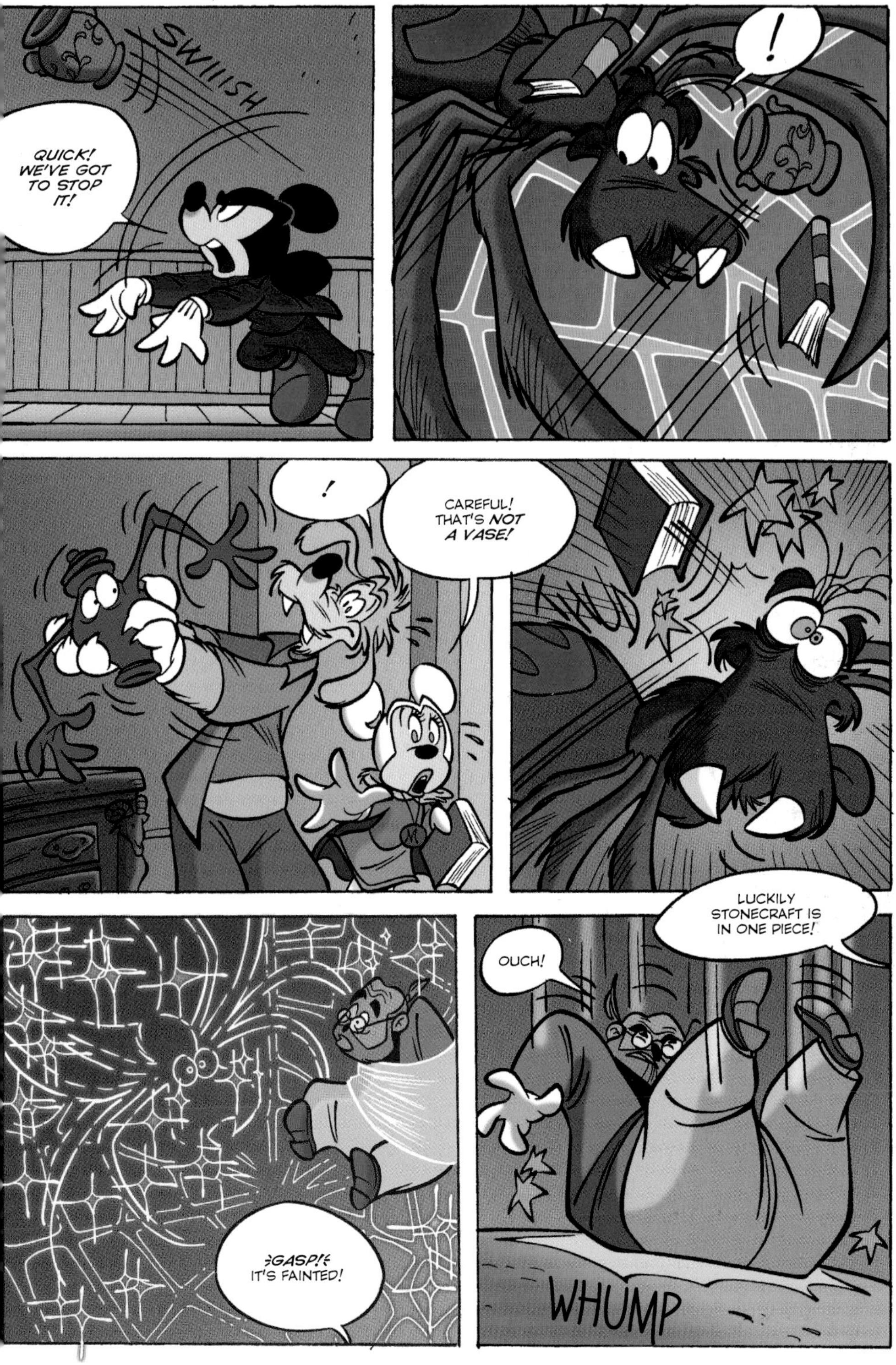

SWIIISH
QUICK! WE'VE GOT TO STOP IT!
!
!
CAREFUL! THAT'S NOT A VASE!
LUCKILY STONECRAFT IS IN ONE PIECE!
OUCH!
GASP! IT'S FAINTED!
WHUMP

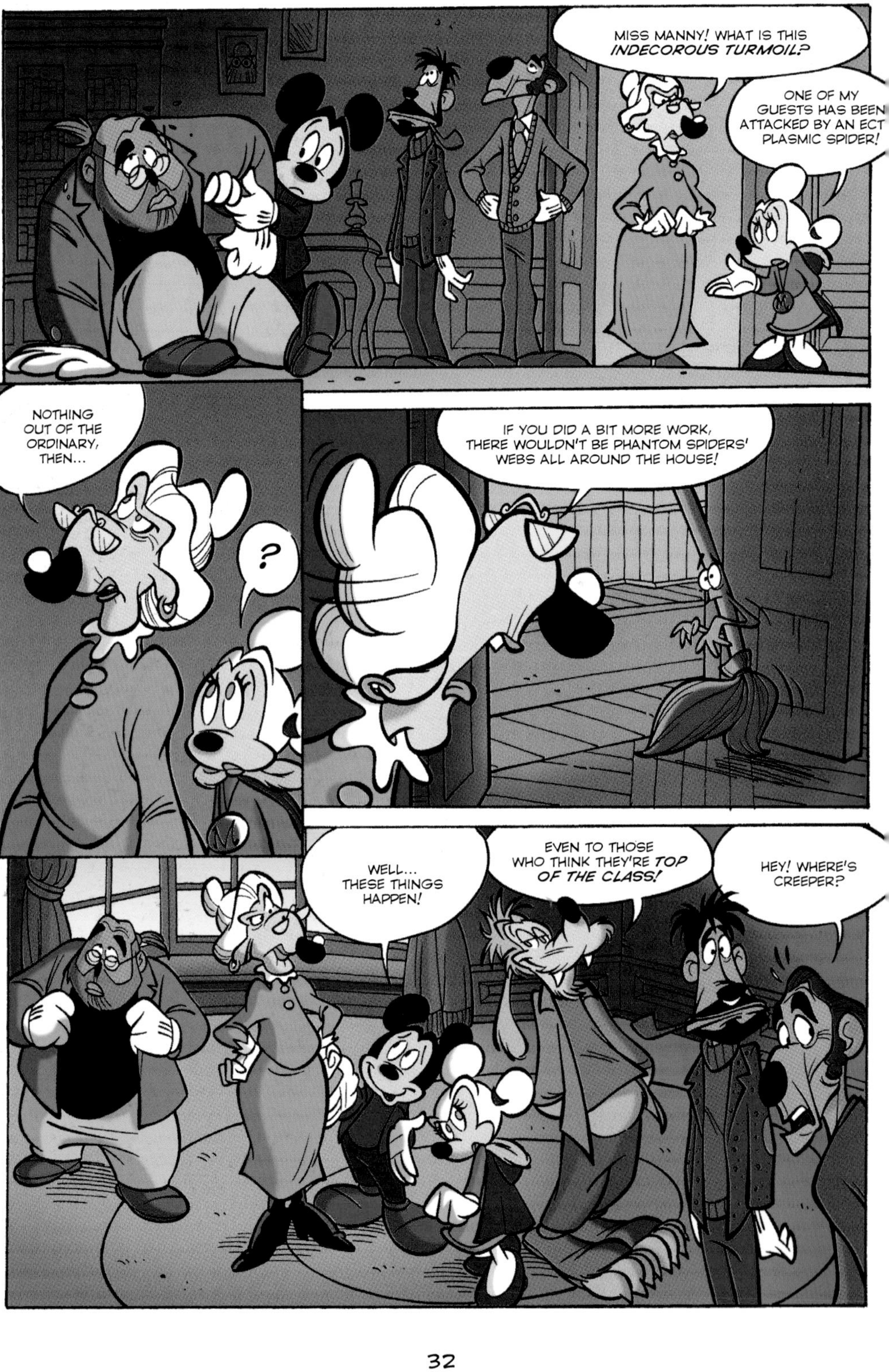
MISS MANNY! WHAT IS THIS INDECOROUS TURMOIL?
ONE OF MY GUESTS HAS BEEN ATTACKED BY AN ECT PLASMIC SPIDER!
NOTHING OUT OF THE ORDINARY, THEN...
?
IF YOU DID A BIT MORE WORK, THERE WOULDN'T BE PHANTOM SPIDERS' WEBS ALL AROUND THE HOUSE!
WELL... THESE THINGS HAPPEN!
EVEN TO THOSE WHO THINK THEY'RE TOP OF THE CLASS!
HEY! WHERE'S CREEPER?

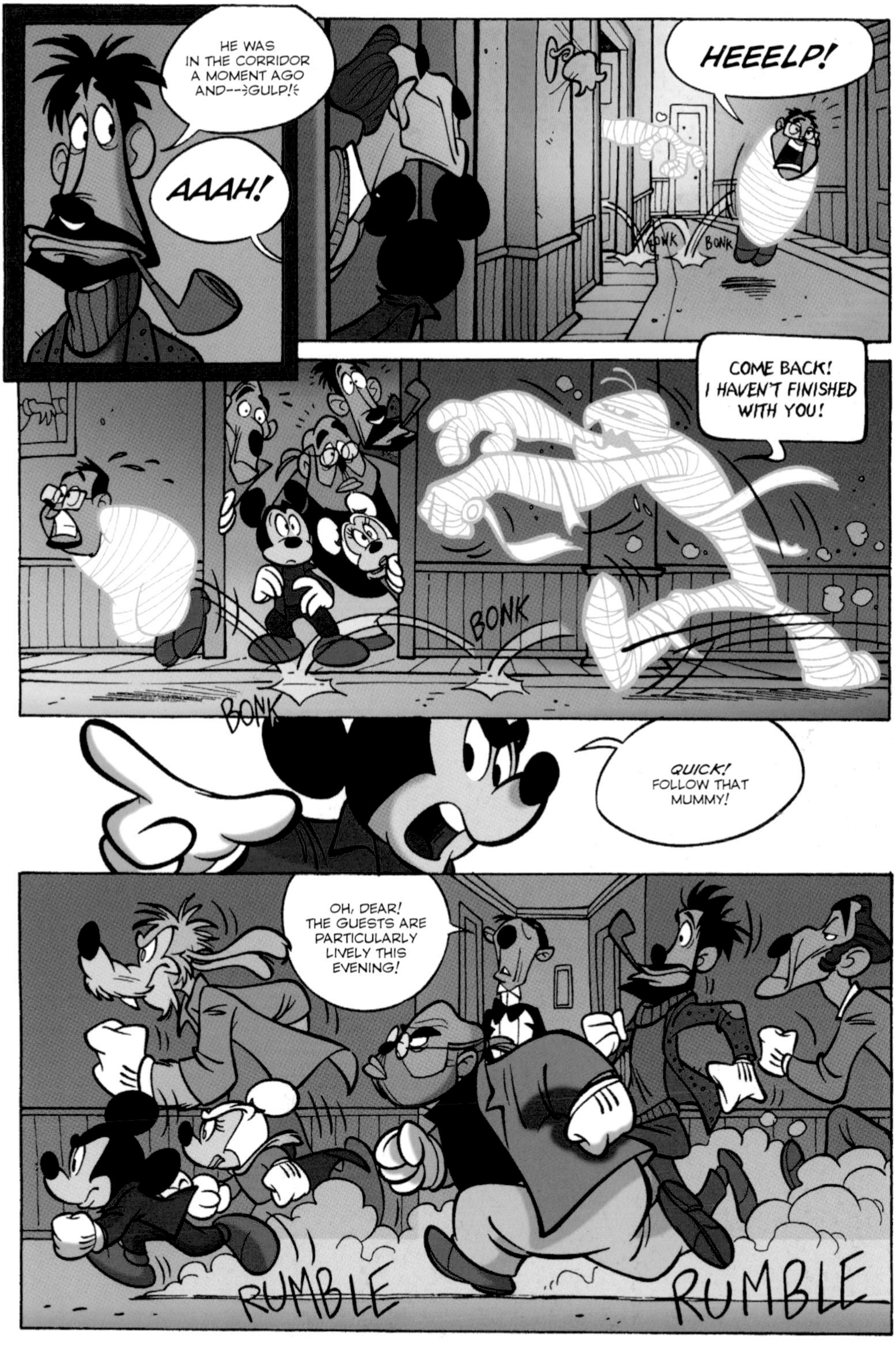
HE WAS IN THE CORRIDOR A MOMENT AGO AND--GULP!
AAAH!
HEEELP!
BONK
BONK
COME BACK! I HAVEN'T FINISHED WITH YOU!
BONK
BONK
QUICK! FOLLOW THAT MUMMY!
OH, DEAR! THE GUESTS ARE PARTICULARLY LIVELY THIS EVENING!
RUMBLE
RUMBLE

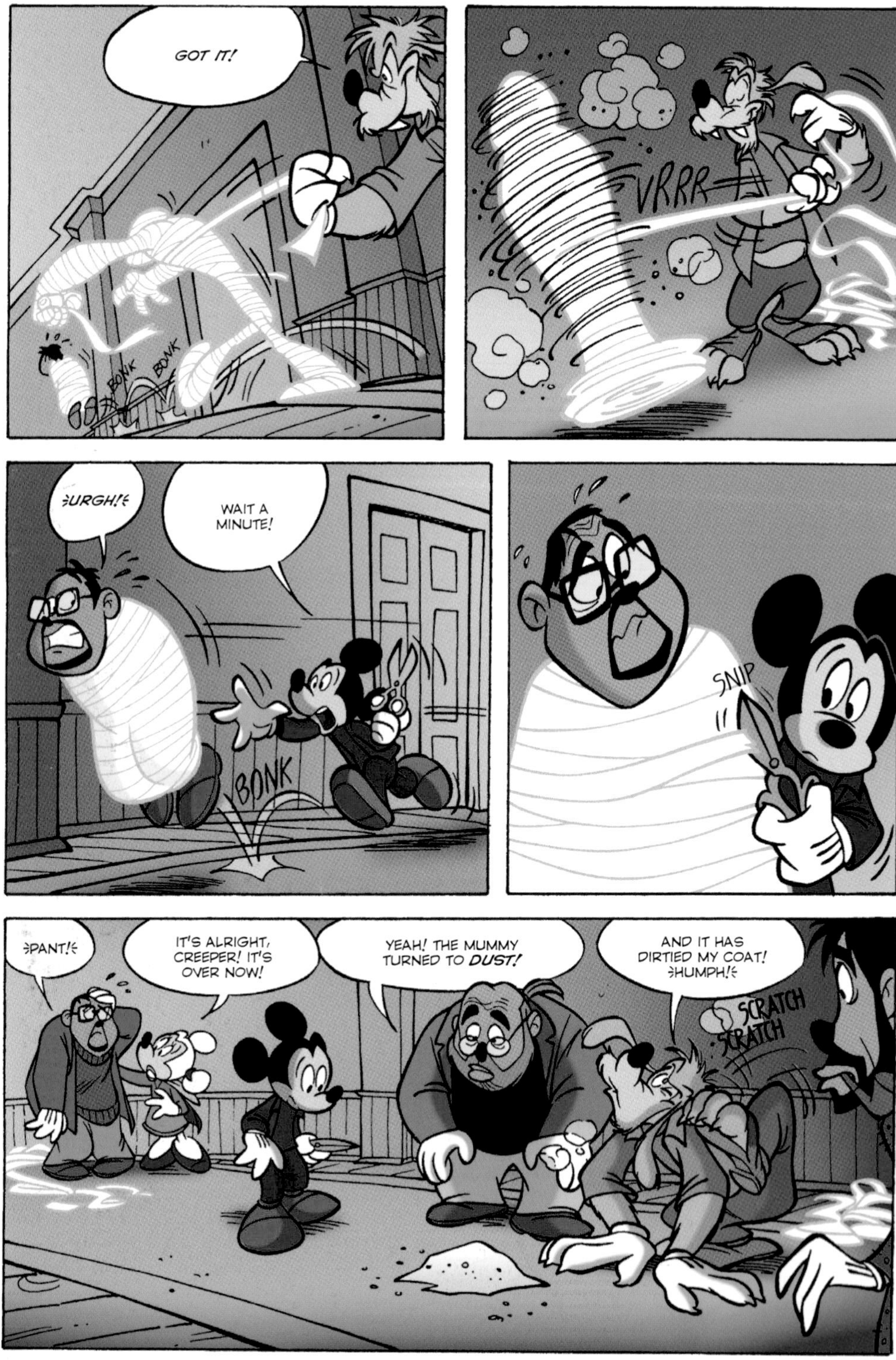
GOT IT!
BONK
BONK
VRRR
URGH!
WAIT A MINUTE!
BONK
SNIP
PANT!
IT'S ALRIGHT, CREEPER! IT'S OVER NOW!
YEAH! THE MUMMY TURNED TO DUST!
AND IT HAS DIRTIED MY COAT! HUMPH!
SCRATCH
SCRATCH

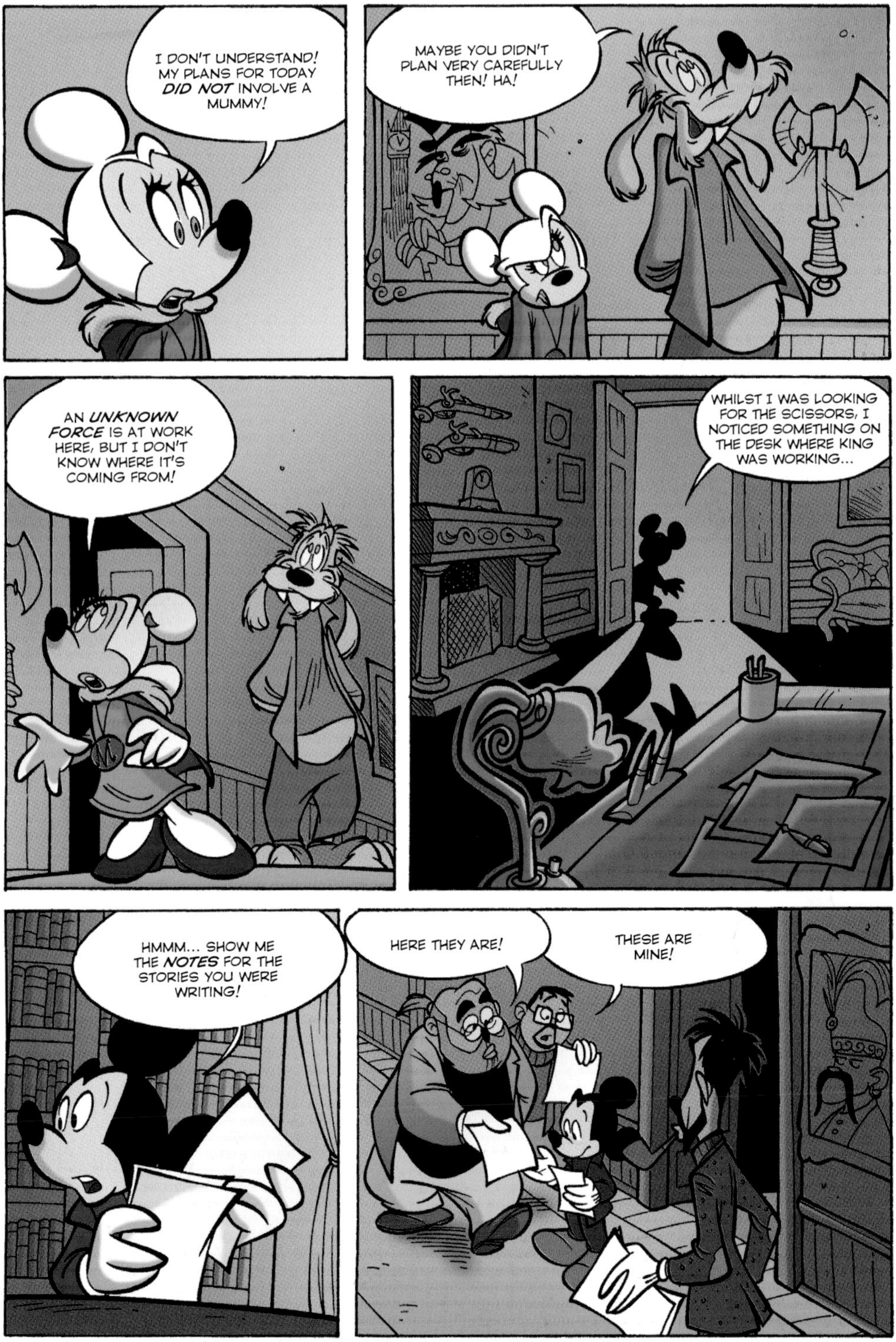
I DON'T UNDERSTAND! MY PLANS FOR TODAY DID NOT INVOLVE A MUMMY!
MAYBE YOU DIDN'T PLAN VERY CAREFULLY THEN! HA!
AN UNKNOWN FORCE IS AT WORK HERE, BUT I DON'T KNOW WHERE IT'S COMING FROM!
WHILST I WAS LOOKING FOR THE SCISSORS, I NOTICED SOMETHING ON THE DESK WHERE KING WAS WORKING...
HMMM... SHOW ME THE NOTES FOR THE STORIES YOU WERE WRITING!
HERE THEY ARE!
THESE ARE MINE!

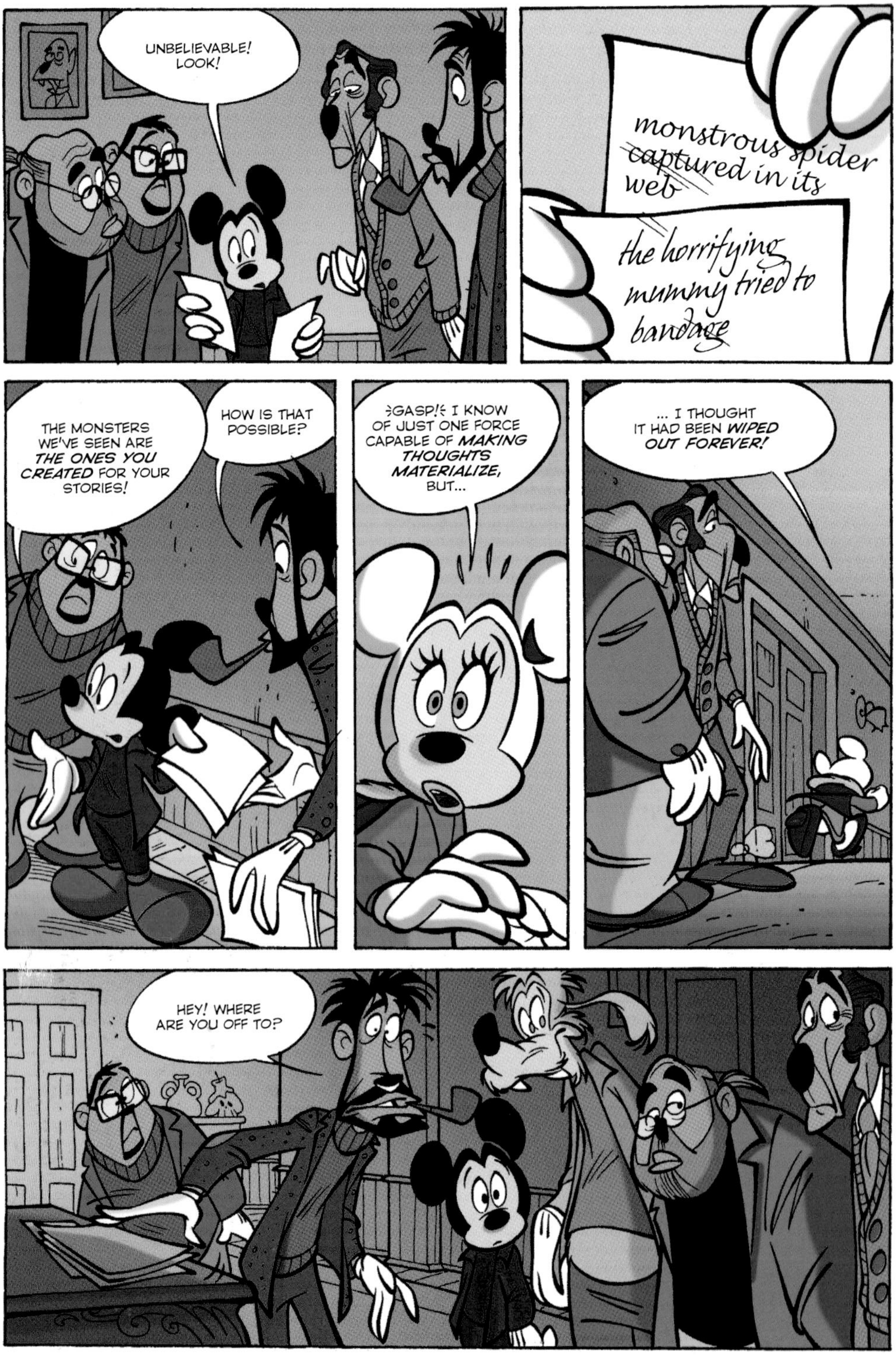
UNBELIEVABLE! LOOK!
monstrous spider captured in its web
the horrifying mummy tried to bandage
THE MONSTERS WE'VE SEEN ARE THE ONES YOU CREATED FOR YOUR STORIES!
HOW IS THAT POSSIBLE?
GASP! I KNOW OF JUST ONE FORCE CAPABLE OF MAKING THOUGHTS MATERIALIZE, BUT...
... I THOUGHT IT HAD BEEN WIPED OUT FOREVER!
HEY! WHERE ARE YOU OFF TO?

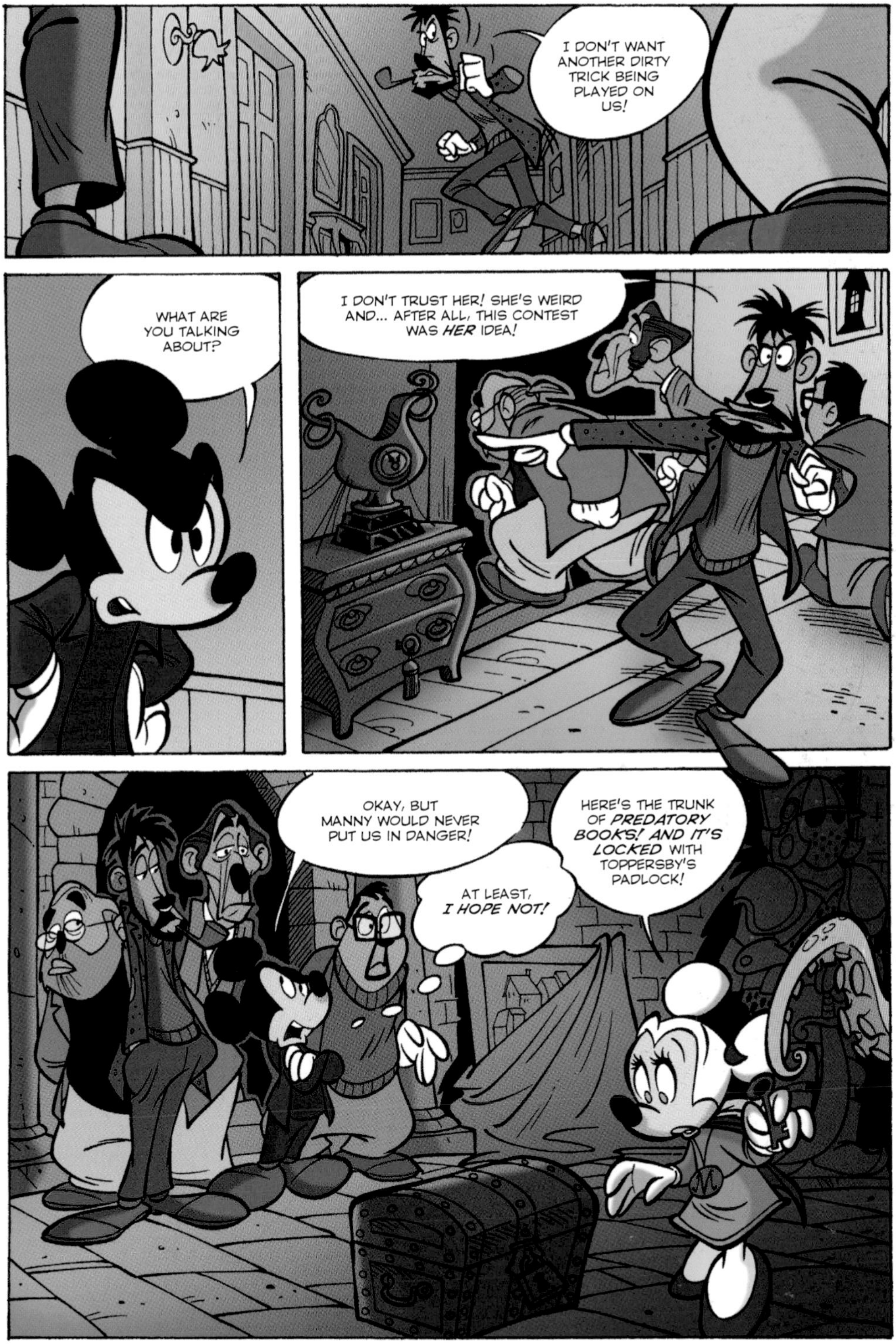
I DON'T WANT ANOTHER DIRTY TRICK BEING PLAYED ON US!
WHAT ARE YOU TALKING ABOUT?
I DON'T TRUST HER! SHE'S WEIRD AND... AFTER ALL, THIS CONTEST WAS *HER* IDEA!
OKAY, BUT MANNY WOULD NEVER PUT US IN DANGER!
AT LEAST, *I HOPE NOT!*
HERE'S THE TRUNK OF *PREDATORY BOOKS! AND IT'S LOCKED* WITH TOPPERSBY'S PADLOCK!

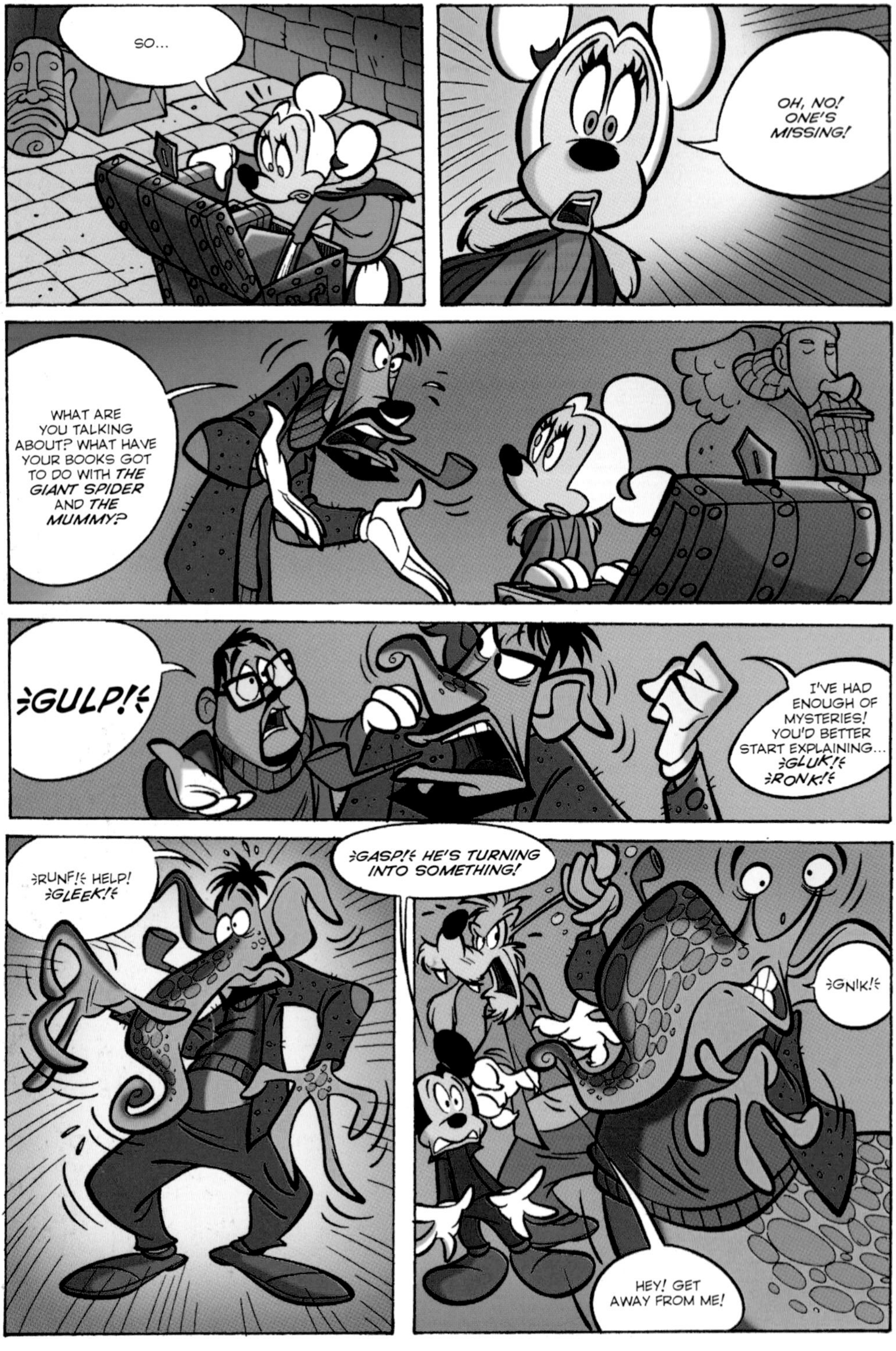

SO...
OH, NO! ONE'S MISSING!
WHAT ARE YOU TALKING ABOUT? WHAT HAVE YOUR BOOKS GOT TO DO WITH THE GIANT SPIDER AND THE MUMMY?
GULP!
I'VE HAD ENOUGH OF MYSTERIES! YOU'D BETTER START EXPLAINING... GLUK! RONK!
RUNF! HELP! GLEEK!
GASP! HE'S TURNING INTO SOMETHING!
GNIK!
HEY! GET AWAY FROM ME!

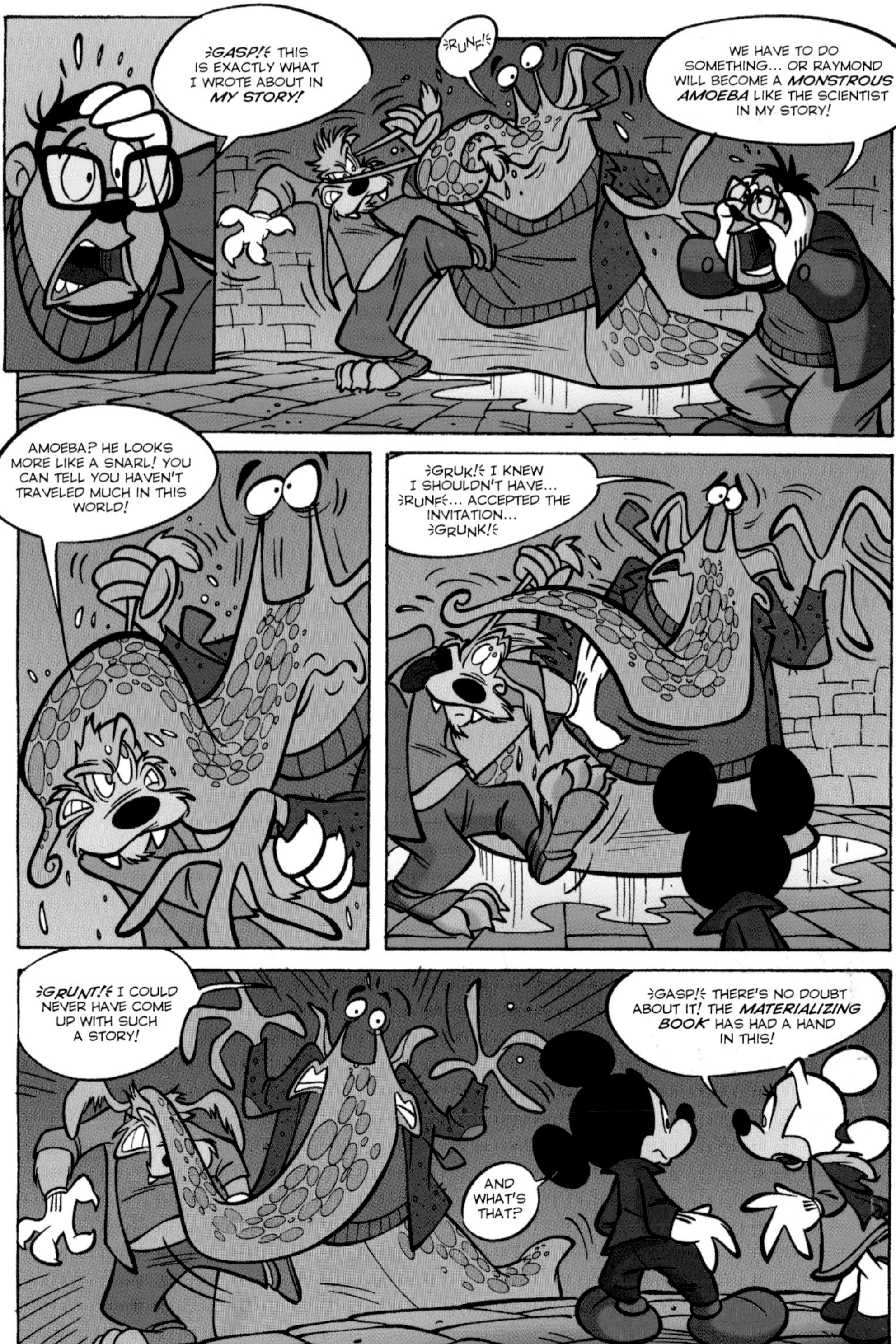
GASP! THIS IS EXACTLY WHAT I WROTE ABOUT IN MY STORY!
RUNF!
WE HAVE TO DO SOMETHING... OR RAYMOND WILL BECOME A MONSTROUS AMOEBA LIKE THE SCIENTIST IN MY STORY!
AMOEBA? HE LOOKS MORE LIKE A SNARL! YOU CAN TELL YOU HAVEN'T TRAVELED MUCH IN THIS WORLD!
GRUK! I KNEW I SHOULDN'T HAVE... RUNF... ACCEPTED THE INVITATION... GRUNK!
GRUNT! I COULD NEVER HAVE COME UP WITH SUCH A STORY!
GASP! THERE'S NO DOUBT ABOUT IT! THE MATERIALIZING BOOK HAS HAD A HAND IN THIS!
AND WHAT'S THAT?

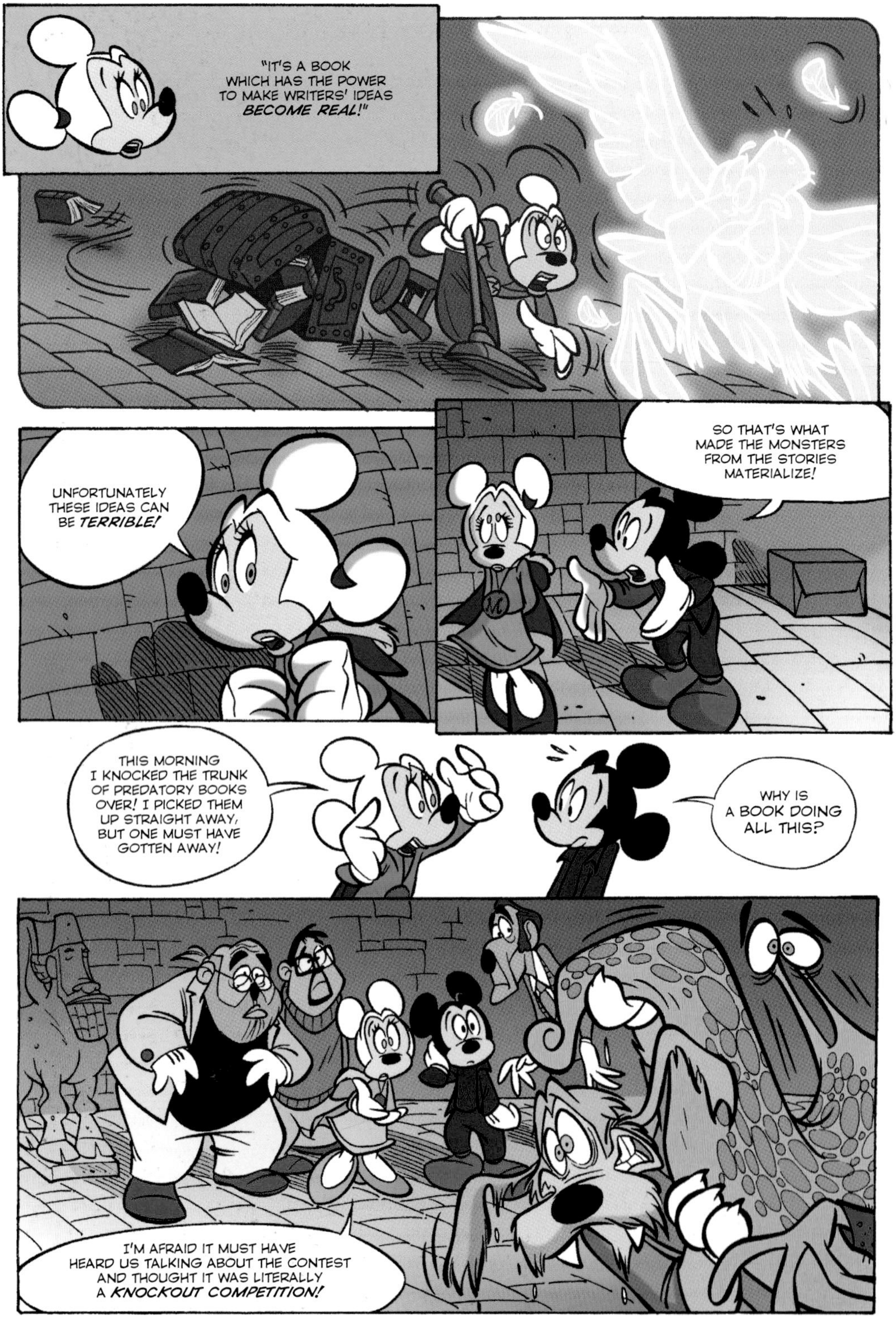
"IT'S A BOOK WHICH HAS THE POWER TO MAKE WRITERS' IDEAS *BECOME REAL!*"
UNFORTUNATELY THESE IDEAS CAN BE *TERRIBLE!*
SO THAT'S WHAT MADE THE MONSTERS FROM THE STORIES MATERIALIZE!
THIS MORNING I KNOCKED THE TRUNK OF PREDATORY BOOKS OVER! I PICKED THEM UP STRAIGHT AWAY, BUT ONE MUST HAVE GOTTEN AWAY!
WHY IS A BOOK DOING ALL THIS?
I'M AFRAID IT MUST HAVE HEARD US TALKING ABOUT THE CONTEST AND THOUGHT IT WAS LITERALLY A *KNOCKOUT COMPETITION!*

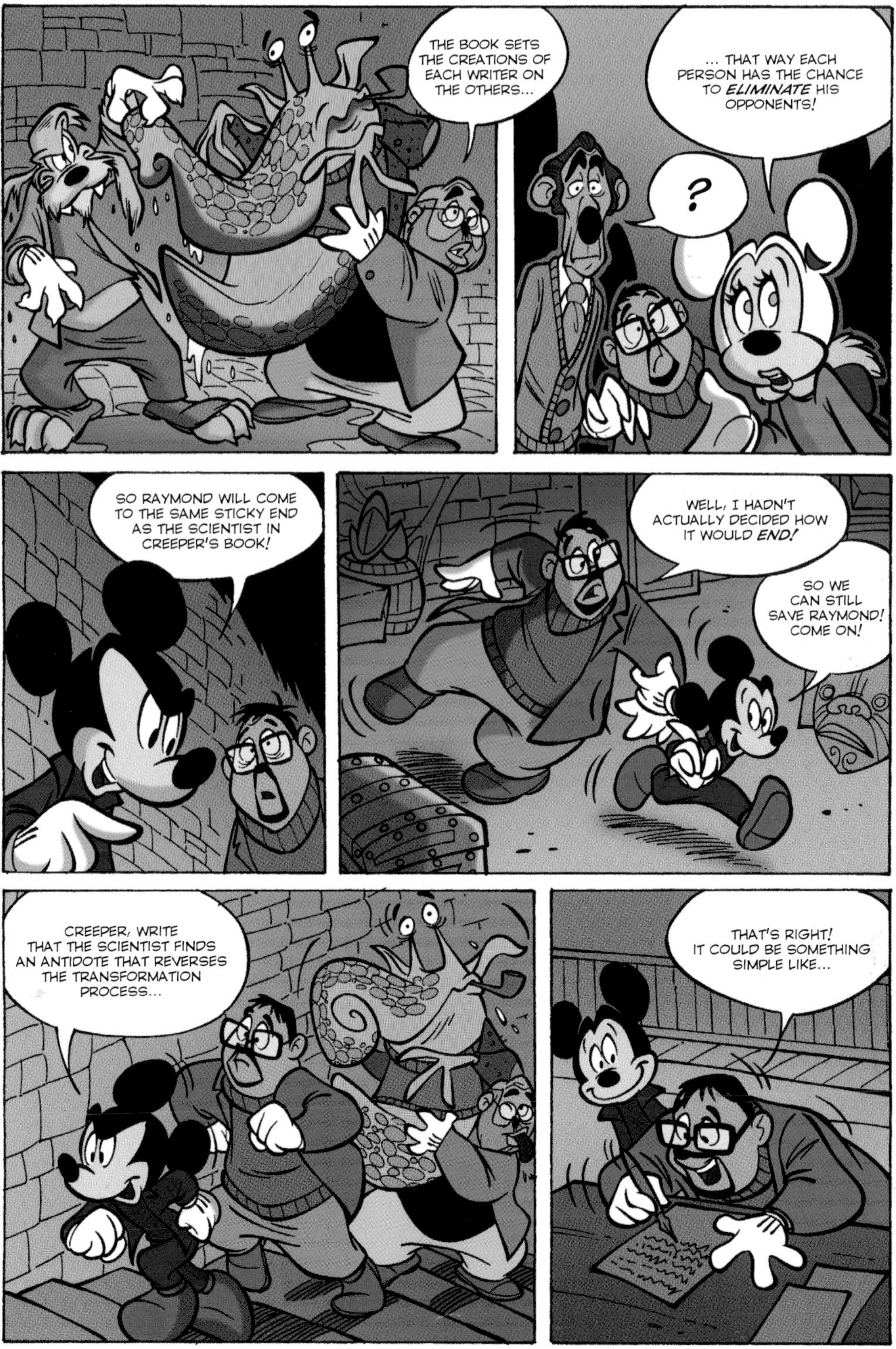
THE BOOK SETS THE CREATIONS OF EACH WRITER ON THE OTHERS...
... THAT WAY EACH PERSON HAS THE CHANCE TO *ELIMINATE* HIS OPPONENTS!
?
SO RAYMOND WILL COME TO THE SAME STICKY END AS THE SCIENTIST IN CREEPER'S BOOK!
WELL, I HADN'T ACTUALLY DECIDED HOW IT WOULD *END!*
SO WE CAN STILL SAVE RAYMOND! COME ON!
CREEPER, WRITE THAT THE SCIENTIST FINDS AN ANTIDOTE THAT REVERSES THE TRANSFORMATION PROCESS...
THAT'S RIGHT! IT COULD BE SOMETHING SIMPLE LIKE...

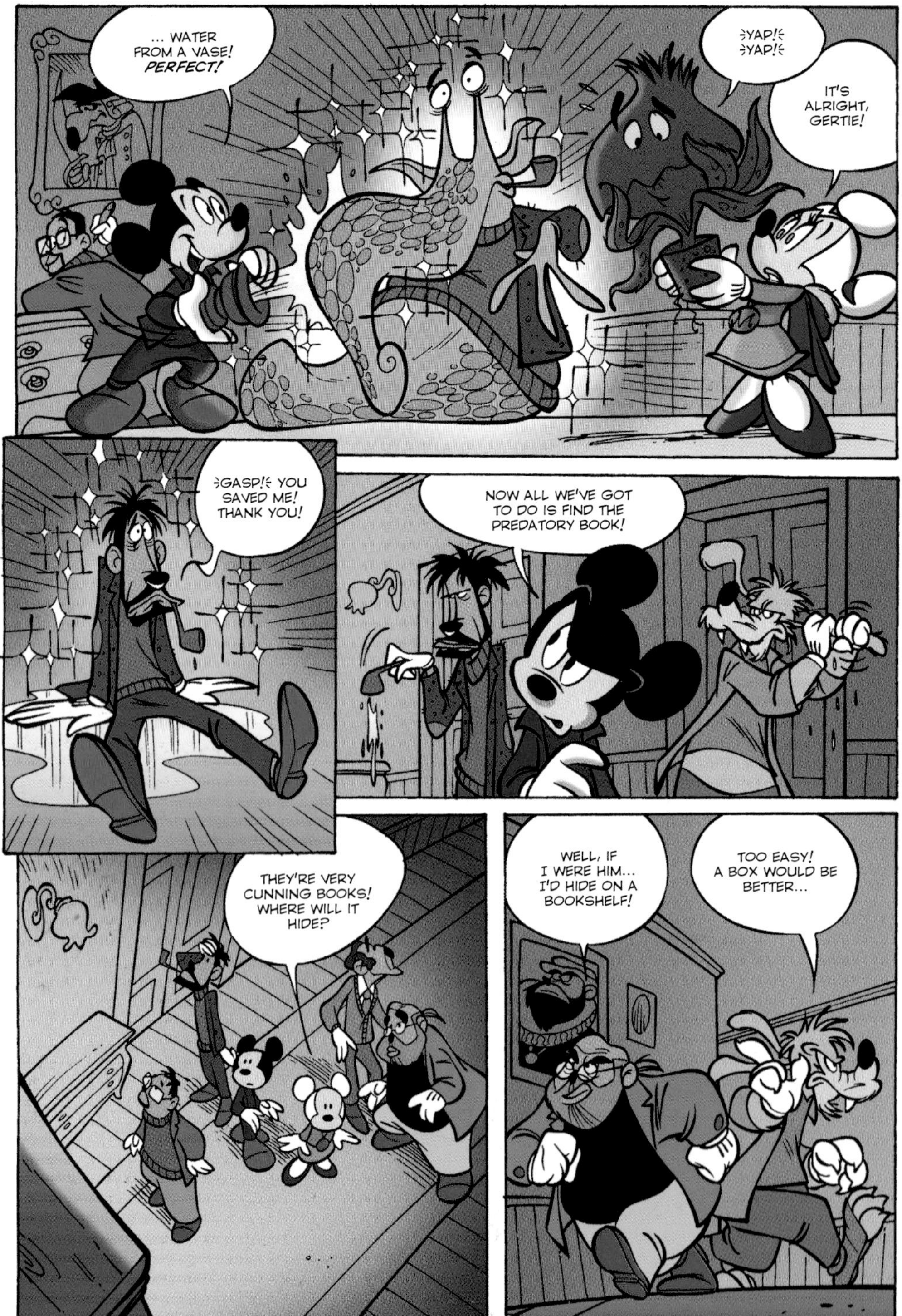
... WATER FROM A VASE! *PERFECT!*
YAP! YAP!
IT'S ALRIGHT, GERTIE!
GASP! YOU SAVED ME! THANK YOU!
NOW ALL WE'VE GOT TO DO IS FIND THE PREDATORY BOOK!
THEY'RE VERY CUNNING BOOKS! WHERE WILL IT HIDE?
WELL, IF I WERE HIM... I'D HIDE ON A BOOKSHELF!
TOO EASY! A BOX WOULD BE BETTER...

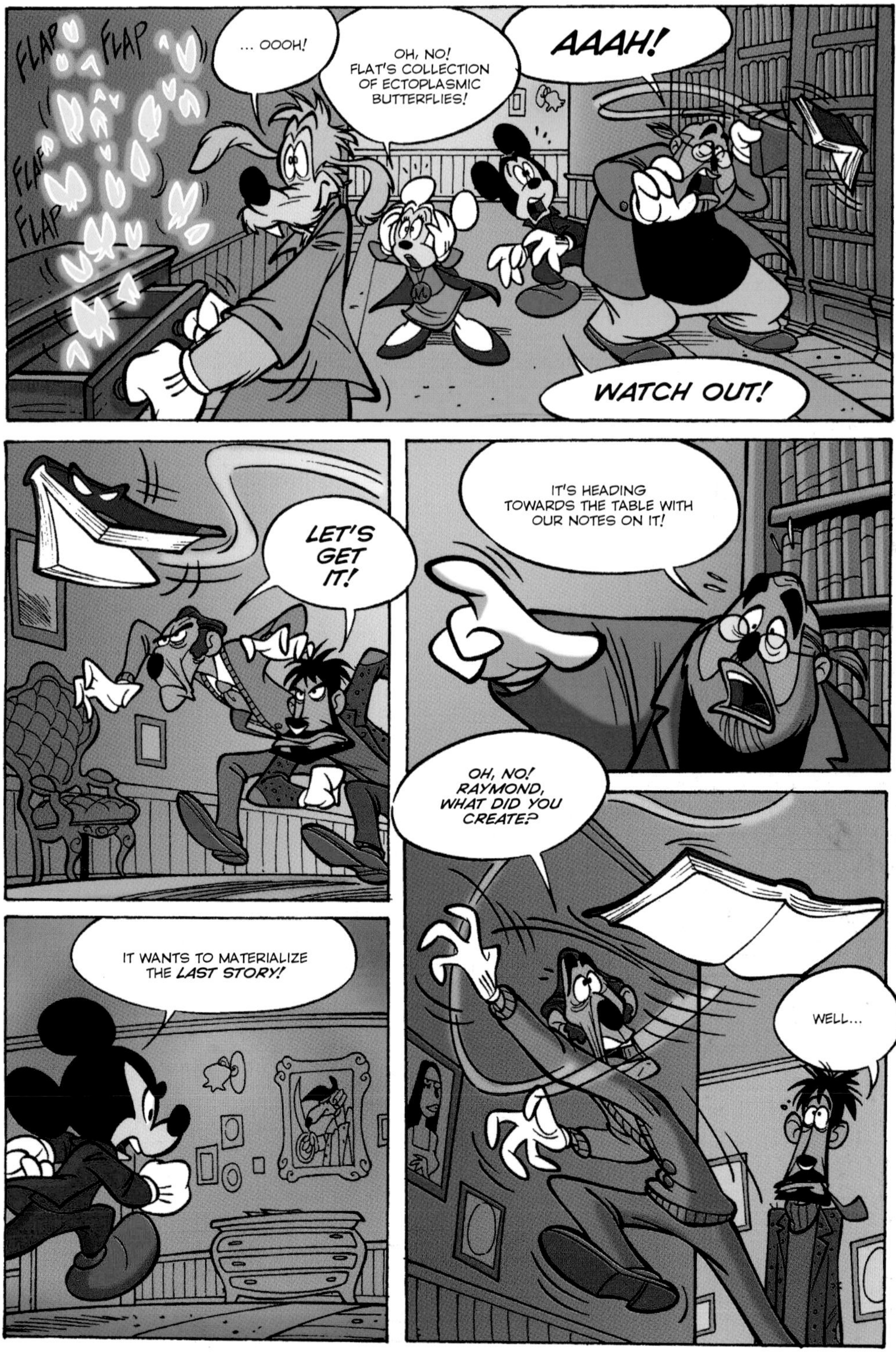
FLAP FLAP
FLAP FLAP
... OOOH!
OH, NO! FLAT'S COLLECTION OF ECTOPLASMIC BUTTERFLIES!
AAAH!
WATCH OUT!
LET'S GET IT!
IT'S HEADING TOWARDS THE TABLE WITH OUR NOTES ON IT!
IT WANTS TO MATERIALIZE THE LAST STORY!
OH, NO! RAYMOND, WHAT DID YOU CREATE?
WELL...

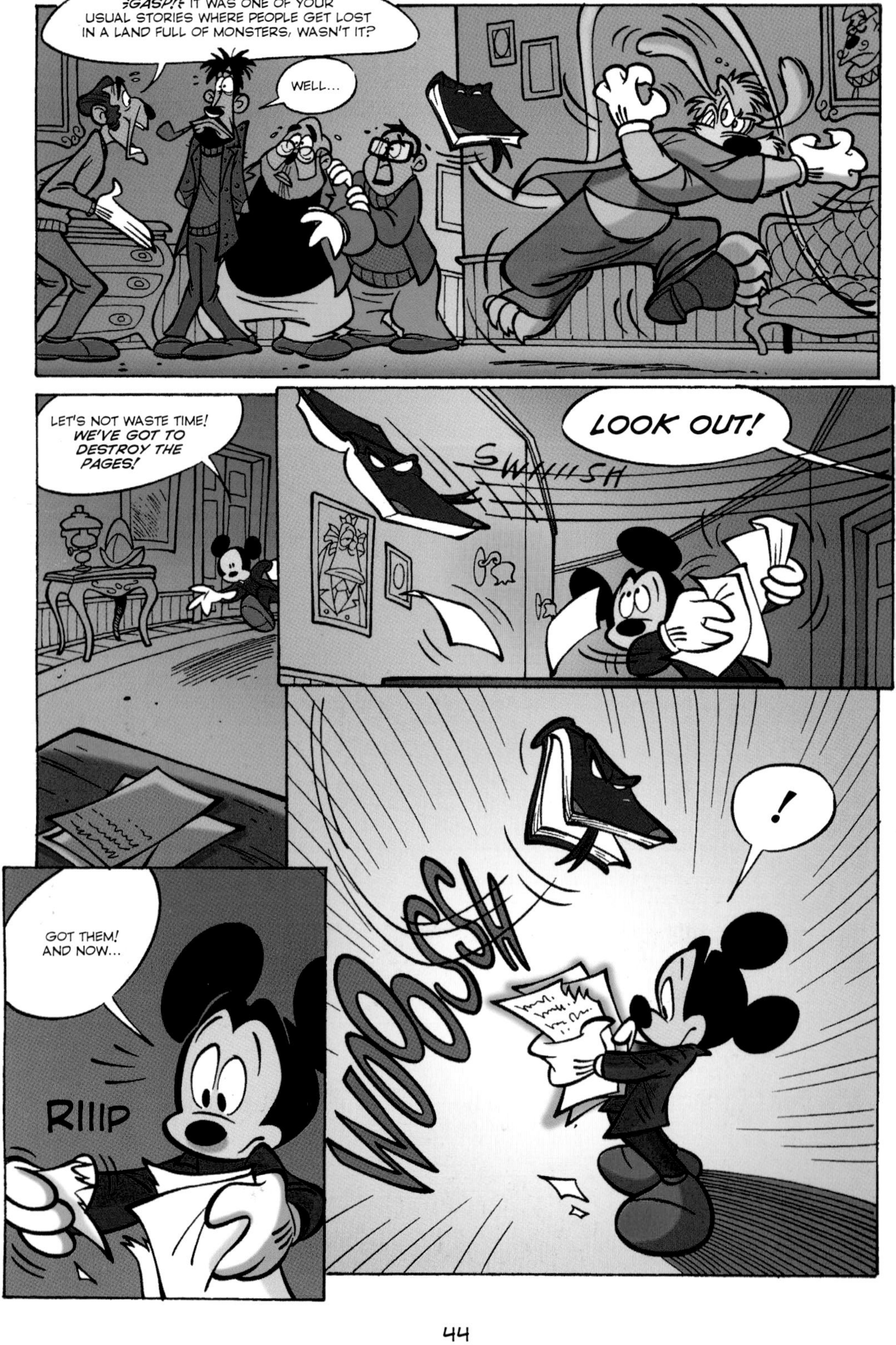

GASP! IT WAS ONE OF YOUR USUAL STORIES WHERE PEOPLE GET LOST IN A LAND FULL OF MONSTERS, WASN'T IT?
WELL...
LET'S NOT WASTE TIME! WE'VE GOT TO DESTROY THE PAGES!
LOOK OUT!
SWHIISH
!
WOOOSH
GOT THEM! AND NOW...
RIIIP

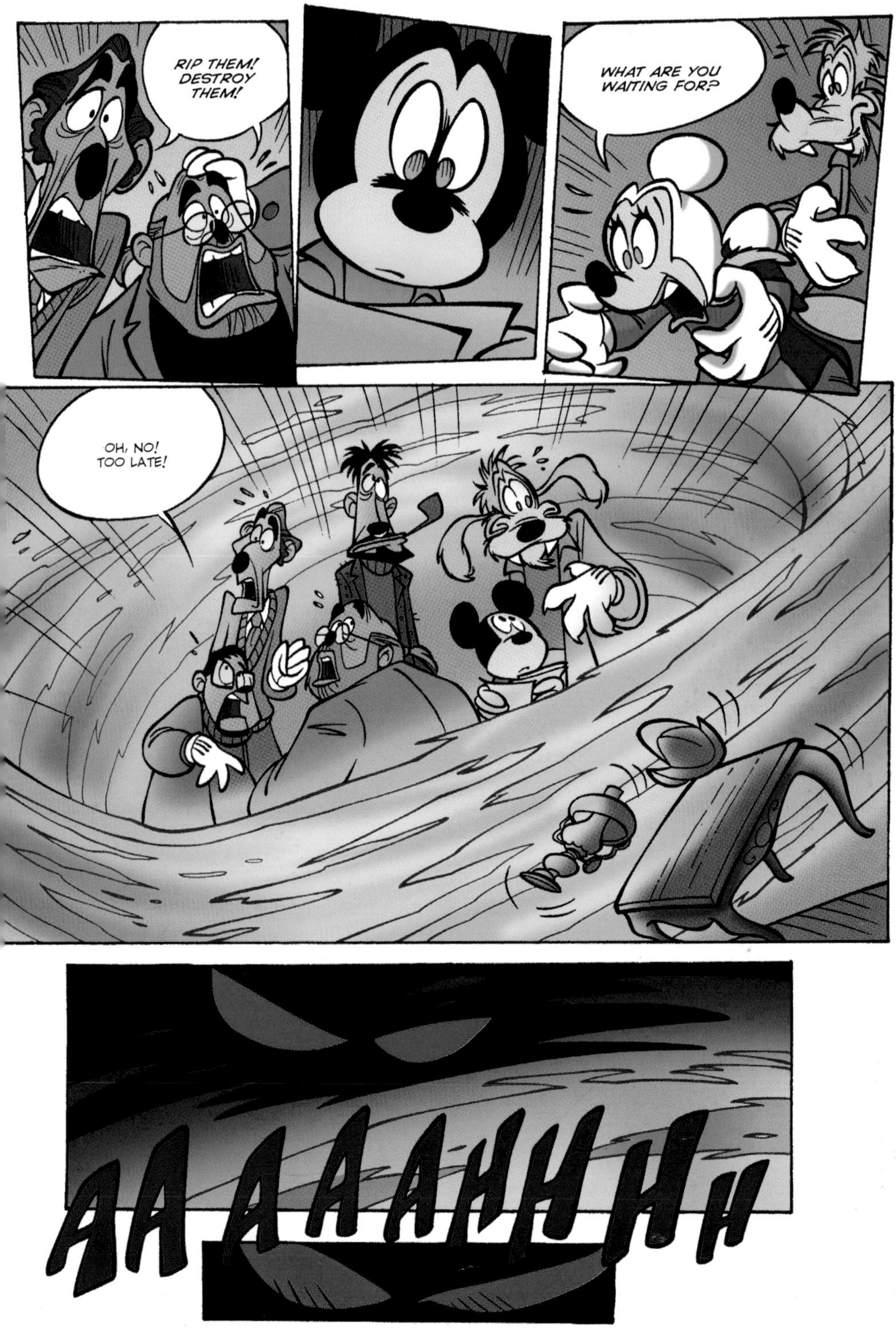
RIP THEM! DESTROY THEM!
WHAT ARE YOU WAITING FOR?
OH, NO! TOO LATE!
AAAAAAHHHHH

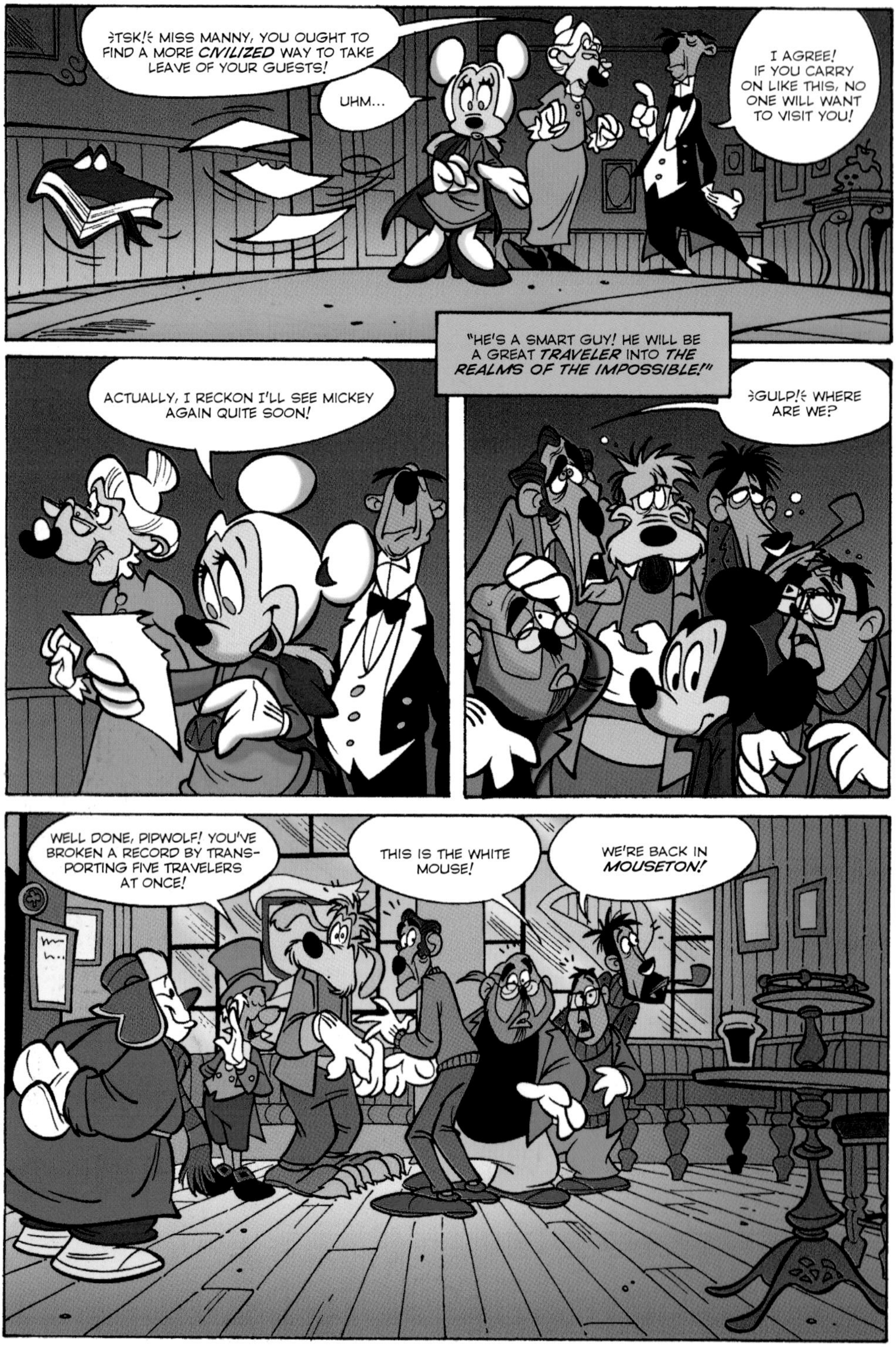
⊰TSK!⊱ MISS MANNY, YOU OUGHT TO FIND A MORE CIVILIZED WAY TO TAKE LEAVE OF YOUR GUESTS!
UHM...
I AGREE! IF YOU CARRY ON LIKE THIS, NO ONE WILL WANT TO VISIT YOU!
ACTUALLY, I RECKON I'LL SEE MICKEY AGAIN QUITE SOON!
"HE'S A SMART GUY! HE WILL BE A GREAT TRAVELER INTO THE REALMS OF THE IMPOSSIBLE!"
⊰GULP!⊱ WHERE ARE WE?
WELL DONE, PIPWOLF! YOU'VE BROKEN A RECORD BY TRANSPORTING FIVE TRAVELERS AT ONCE!
THIS IS THE WHITE MOUSE!
WE'RE BACK IN MOUSETON!

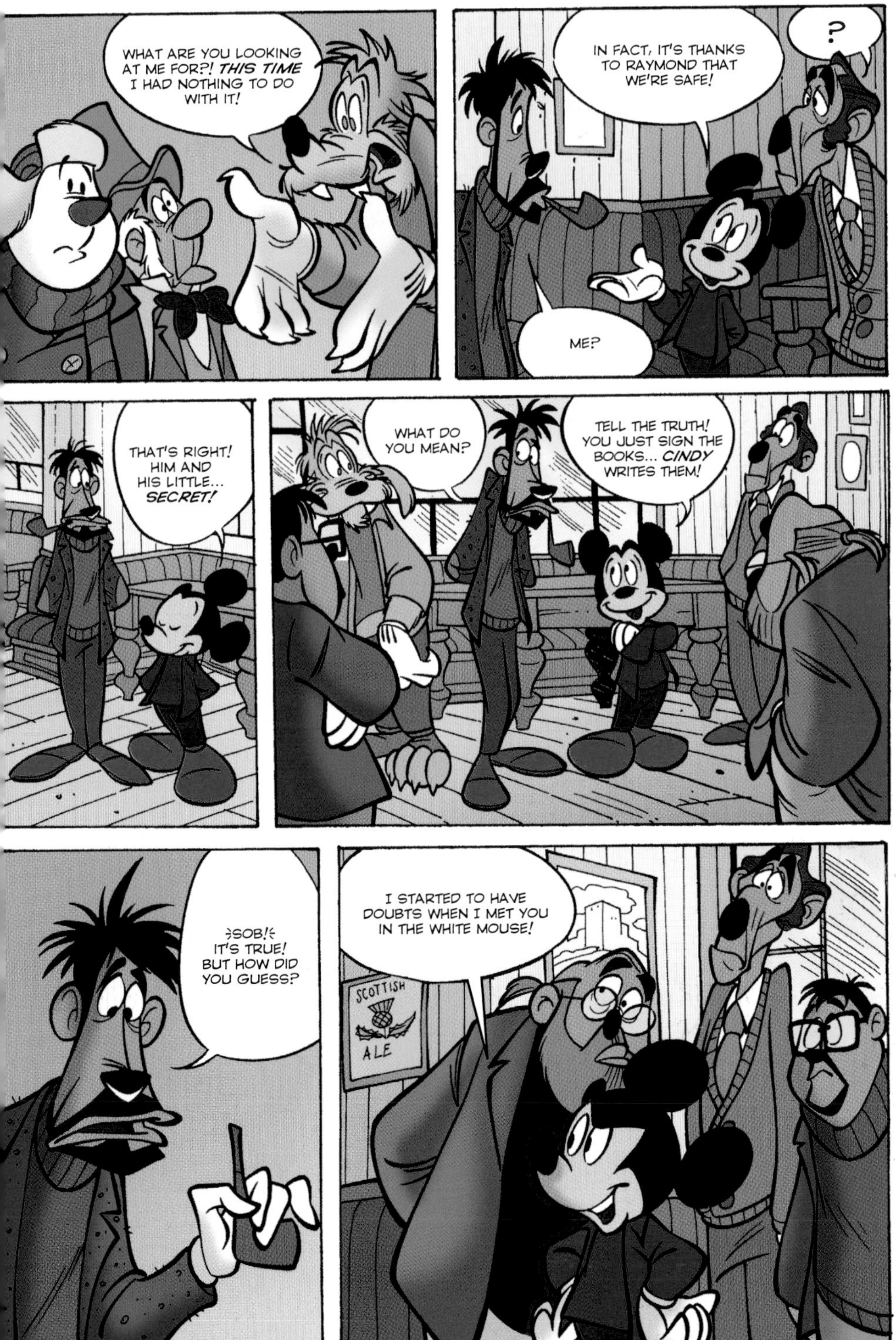
WHAT ARE YOU LOOKING AT ME FOR?! THIS TIME I HAD NOTHING TO DO WITH IT!
IN FACT, IT'S THANKS TO RAYMOND THAT WE'RE SAFE!
?
ME?
THAT'S RIGHT! HIM AND HIS LITTLE... SECRET!
WHAT DO YOU MEAN?
TELL THE TRUTH! YOU JUST SIGN THE BOOKS... CINDY WRITES THEM!
SOB! IT'S TRUE! BUT HOW DID YOU GUESS?
I STARTED TO HAVE DOUBTS WHEN I MET YOU IN THE WHITE MOUSE!
SCOTTISH ALE

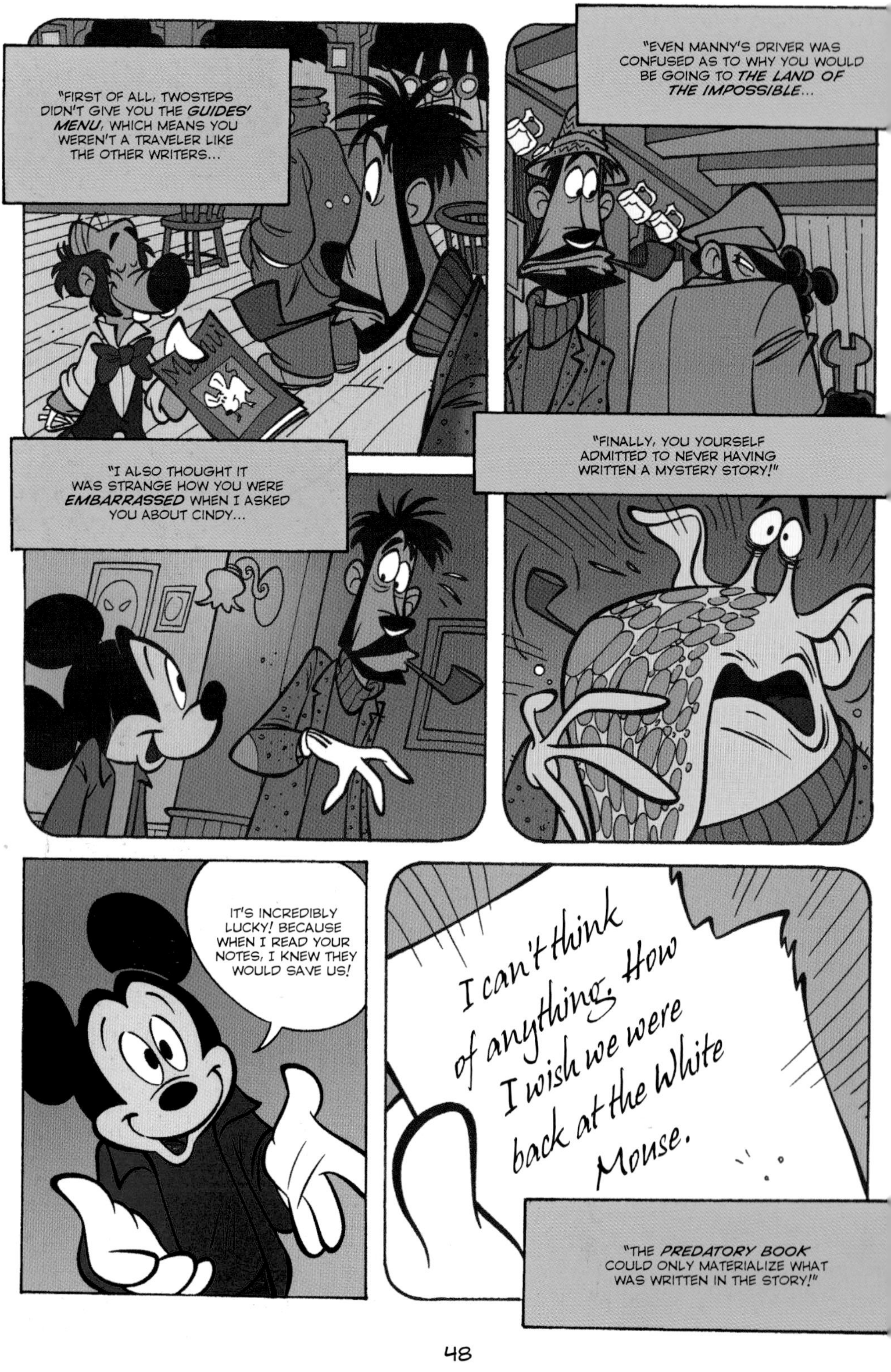
"FIRST OF ALL, TWOSTEPS DIDN'T GIVE YOU THE *GUIDES' MENU*, WHICH MEANS YOU WEREN'T A TRAVELER LIKE THE OTHER WRITERS...
"EVEN MANNY'S DRIVER WAS CONFUSED AS TO WHY YOU WOULD BE GOING TO *THE LAND OF THE IMPOSSIBLE*...
"I ALSO THOUGHT IT WAS STRANGE HOW YOU WERE *EMBARRASSED* WHEN I ASKED YOU ABOUT CINDY...
"FINALLY, YOU YOURSELF ADMITTED TO NEVER HAVING WRITTEN A MYSTERY STORY!"
IT'S INCREDIBLY LUCKY! BECAUSE WHEN I READ YOUR NOTES, I KNEW THEY WOULD SAVE US!
I can't think of anything. How I wish we were back at the White Mouse.
"THE *PREDATORY BOOK* COULD ONLY MATERIALIZE WHAT WAS WRITTEN IN THE STORY!"

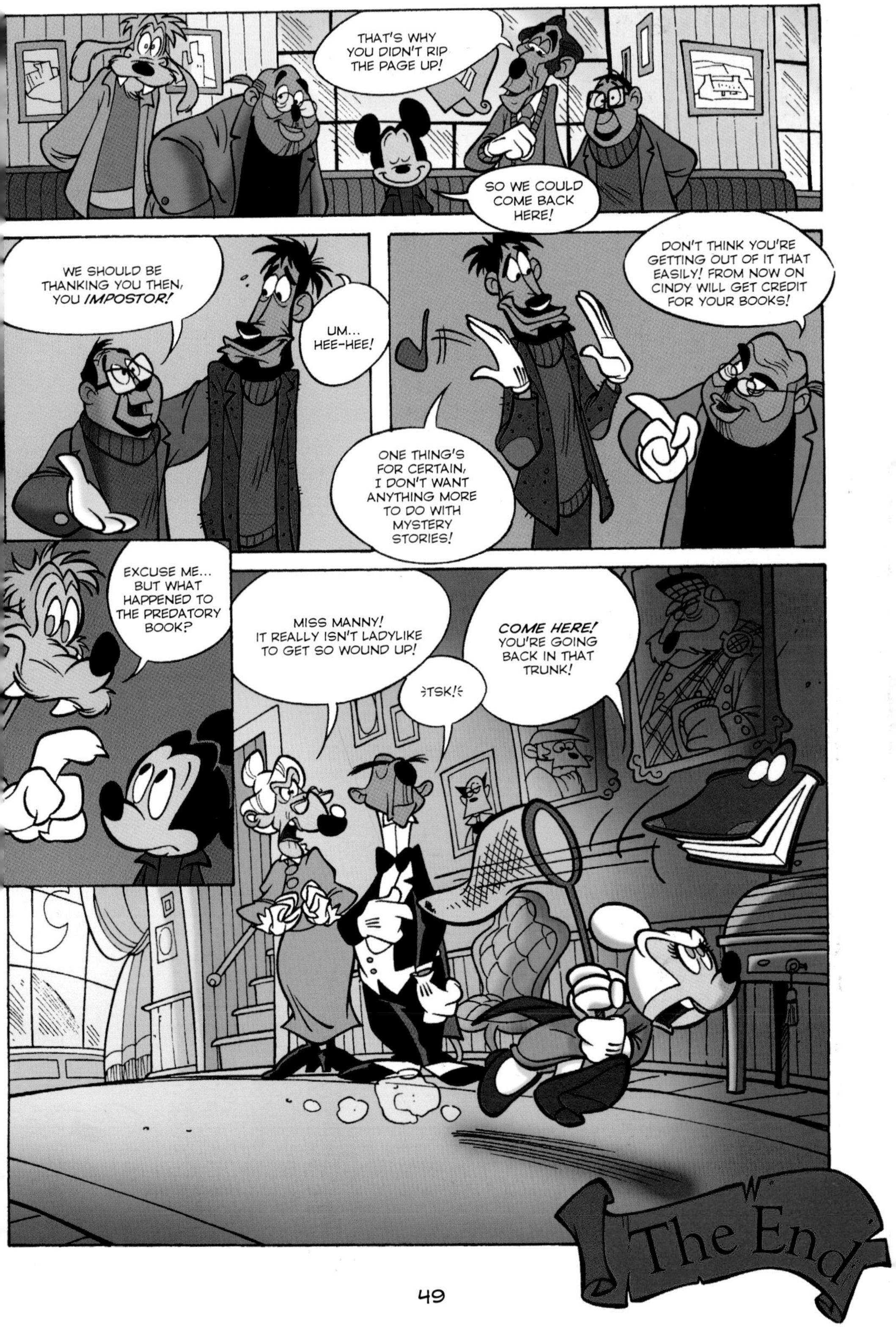
THAT'S WHY YOU DIDN'T RIP THE PAGE UP!
SO WE COULD COME BACK HERE!
WE SHOULD BE THANKING YOU THEN, YOU *IMPOSTOR!*
UM... HEE-HEE!
DON'T THINK YOU'RE GETTING OUT OF IT THAT EASILY! FROM NOW ON CINDY WILL GET CREDIT FOR YOUR BOOKS!
ONE THING'S FOR CERTAIN, I DON'T WANT ANYTHING MORE TO DO WITH MYSTERY STORIES!
EXCUSE ME... BUT WHAT HAPPENED TO THE PREDATORY BOOK?
MISS MANNY! IT REALLY ISN'T LADYLIKE TO GET SO WOUND UP!
TSK!
COME HERE! YOU'RE GOING BACK IN THAT TRUNK!
The End

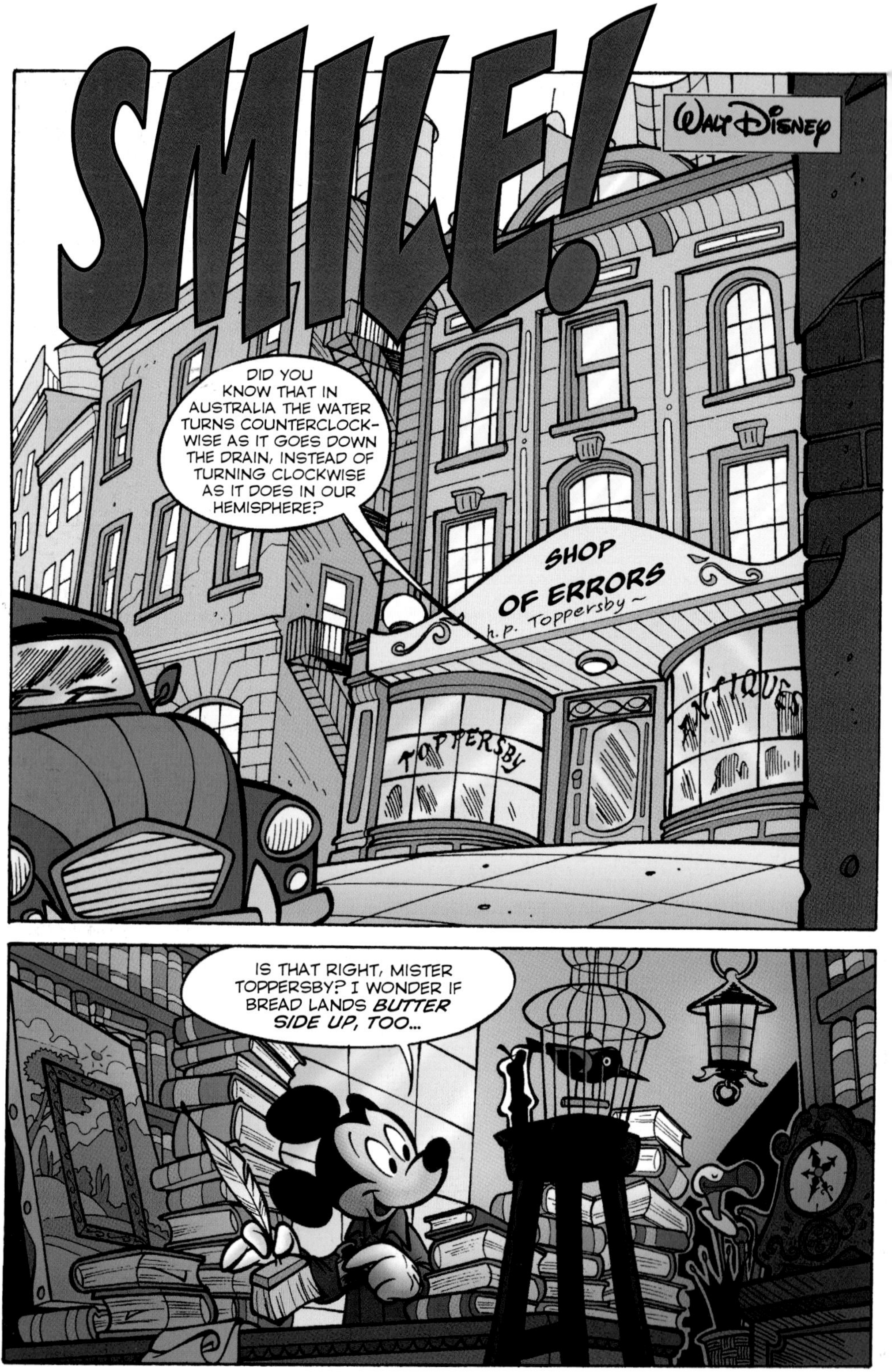
SMILE!
WALT DISNEY
DID YOU KNOW THAT IN AUSTRALIA THE WATER TURNS COUNTERCLOCK-WISE AS IT GOES DOWN THE DRAIN, INSTEAD OF TURNING CLOCKWISE AS IT DOES IN OUR HEMISPHERE?
SHOP OF ERRORS
~h.p. Toppersby~
TOPPERSBY
ANTIQUES
IS THAT RIGHT, MISTER TOPPERSBY? I WONDER IF BREAD LANDS *BUTTER SIDE UP*, TOO...

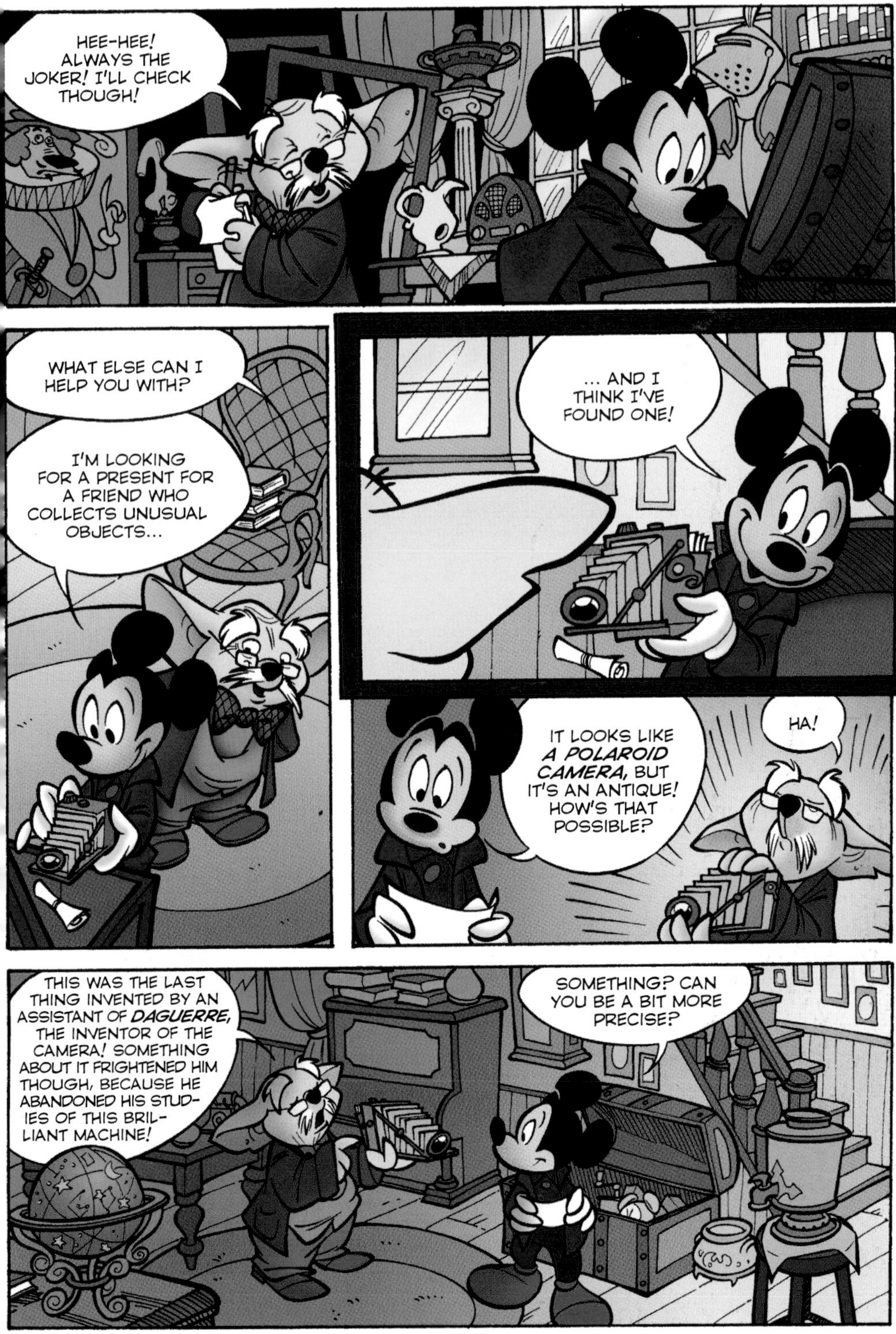
HEE-HEE! ALWAYS THE JOKER! I'LL CHECK THOUGH!
WHAT ELSE CAN I HELP YOU WITH?
I'M LOOKING FOR A PRESENT FOR A FRIEND WHO COLLECTS UNUSUAL OBJECTS...
... AND I THINK I'VE FOUND ONE!
IT LOOKS LIKE *A POLAROID CAMERA,* BUT IT'S AN ANTIQUE! HOW'S THAT POSSIBLE?
HA!
THIS WAS THE LAST THING INVENTED BY AN ASSISTANT OF *DAGUERRE,* THE INVENTOR OF THE CAMERA! SOMETHING ABOUT IT FRIGHTENED HIM THOUGH, BECAUSE HE ABANDONED HIS STUDIES OF THIS BRILLIANT MACHINE!
SOMETHING? CAN YOU BE A BIT MORE PRECISE?

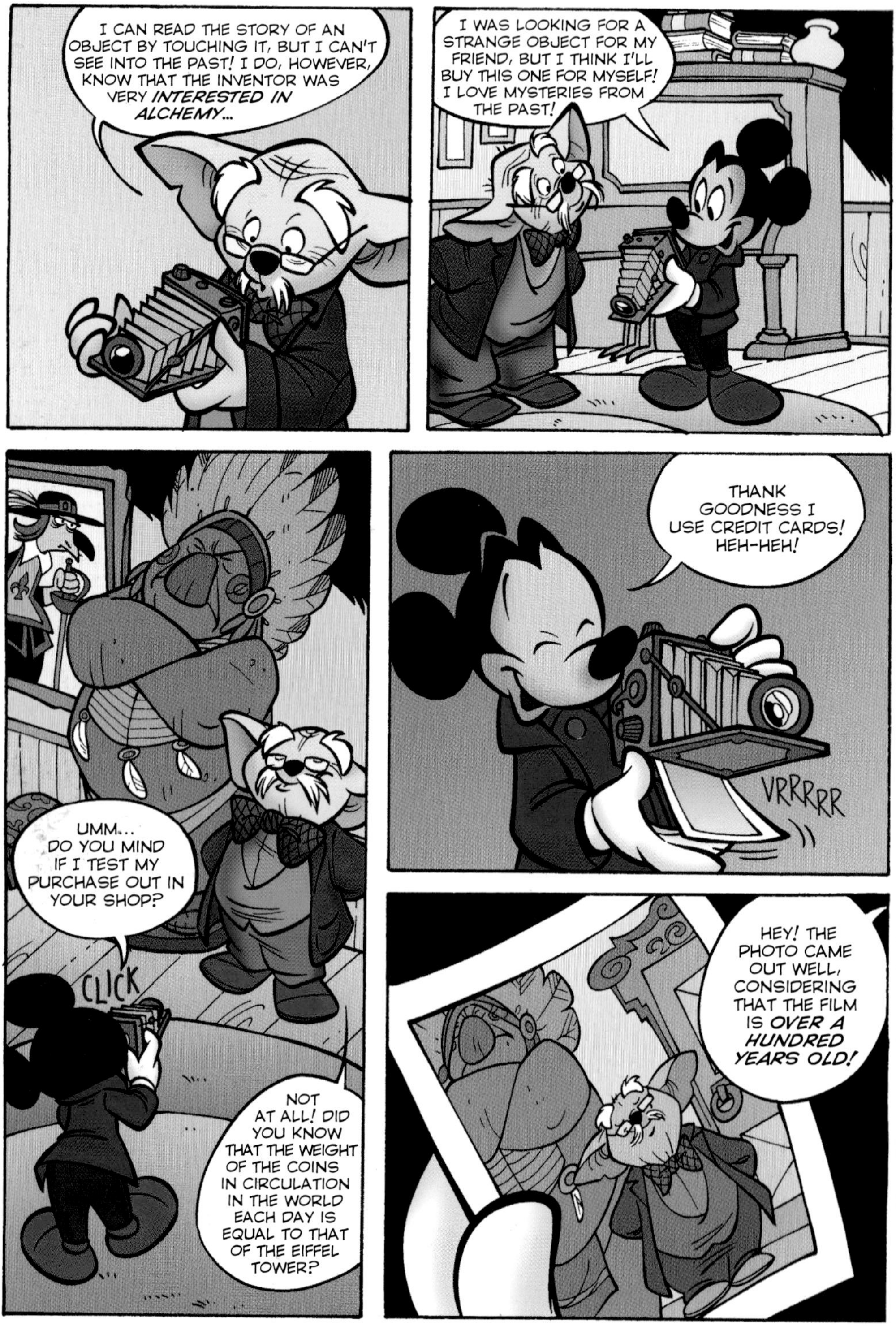
I CAN READ THE STORY OF AN OBJECT BY TOUCHING IT, BUT I CAN'T SEE INTO THE PAST! I DO, HOWEVER, KNOW THAT THE INVENTOR WAS VERY *INTERESTED IN ALCHEMY*...
I WAS LOOKING FOR A STRANGE OBJECT FOR MY FRIEND, BUT I THINK I'LL BUY THIS ONE FOR MYSELF! I LOVE MYSTERIES FROM THE PAST!
UMM... DO YOU MIND IF I TEST MY PURCHASE OUT IN YOUR SHOP?
CLICK
NOT AT ALL! DID YOU KNOW THAT THE WEIGHT OF THE COINS IN CIRCULATION IN THE WORLD EACH DAY IS EQUAL TO THAT OF THE EIFFEL TOWER?
THANK GOODNESS I USE CREDIT CARDS! HEH-HEH!
VRRRRR
HEY! THE PHOTO CAME OUT WELL, CONSIDERING THAT THE FILM IS *OVER A HUNDRED YEARS OLD!*

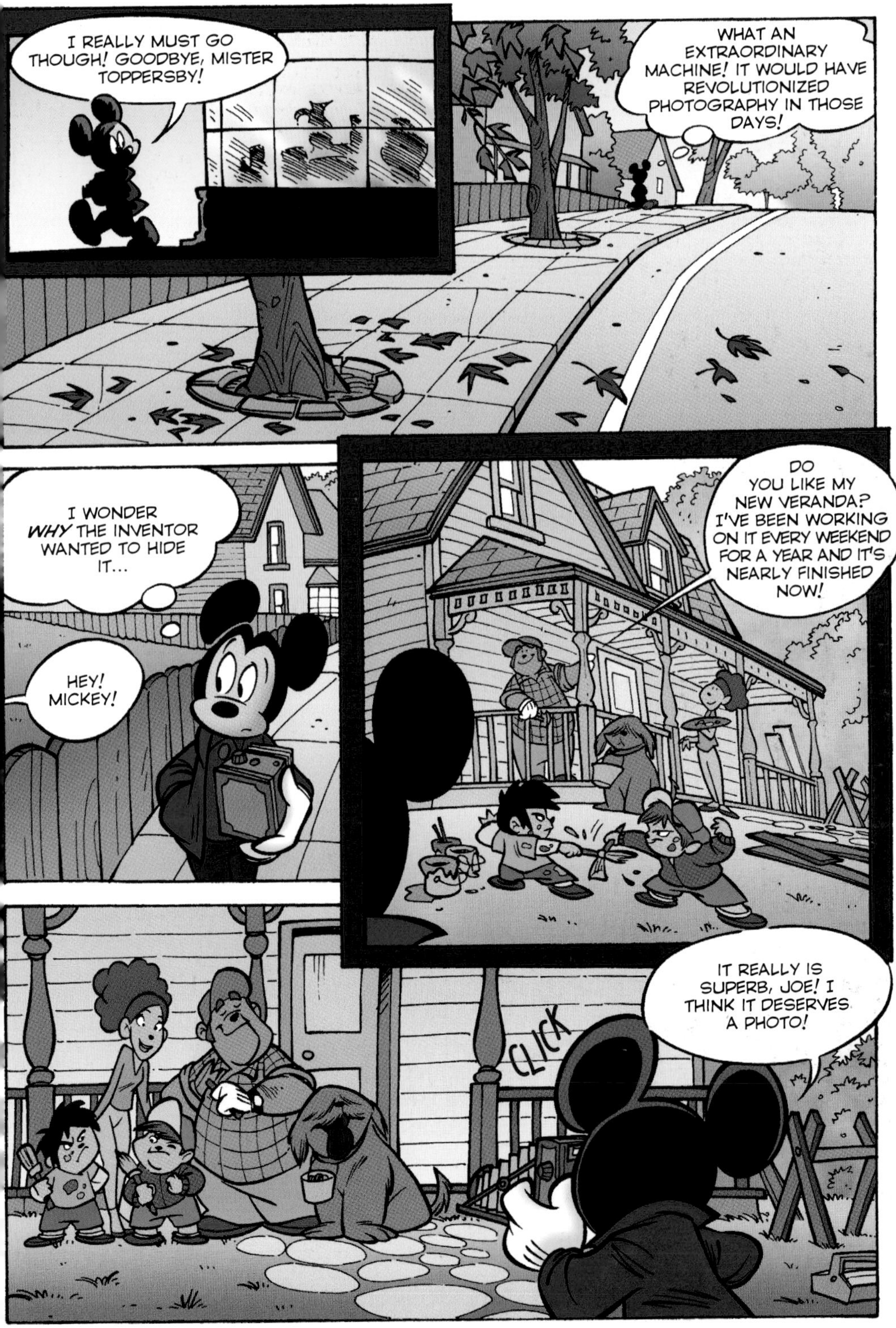
I REALLY MUST GO THOUGH! GOODBYE, MISTER TOPPERSBY!
WHAT AN EXTRAORDINARY MACHINE! IT WOULD HAVE REVOLUTIONIZED PHOTOGRAPHY IN THOSE DAYS!
I WONDER *WHY* THE INVENTOR WANTED TO HIDE IT...
HEY! MICKEY!
DO YOU LIKE MY NEW VERANDA? I'VE BEEN WORKING ON IT EVERY WEEKEND FOR A YEAR AND IT'S NEARLY FINISHED NOW!
IT REALLY IS SUPERB, JOE! I THINK IT DESERVES A PHOTO!
CLICK

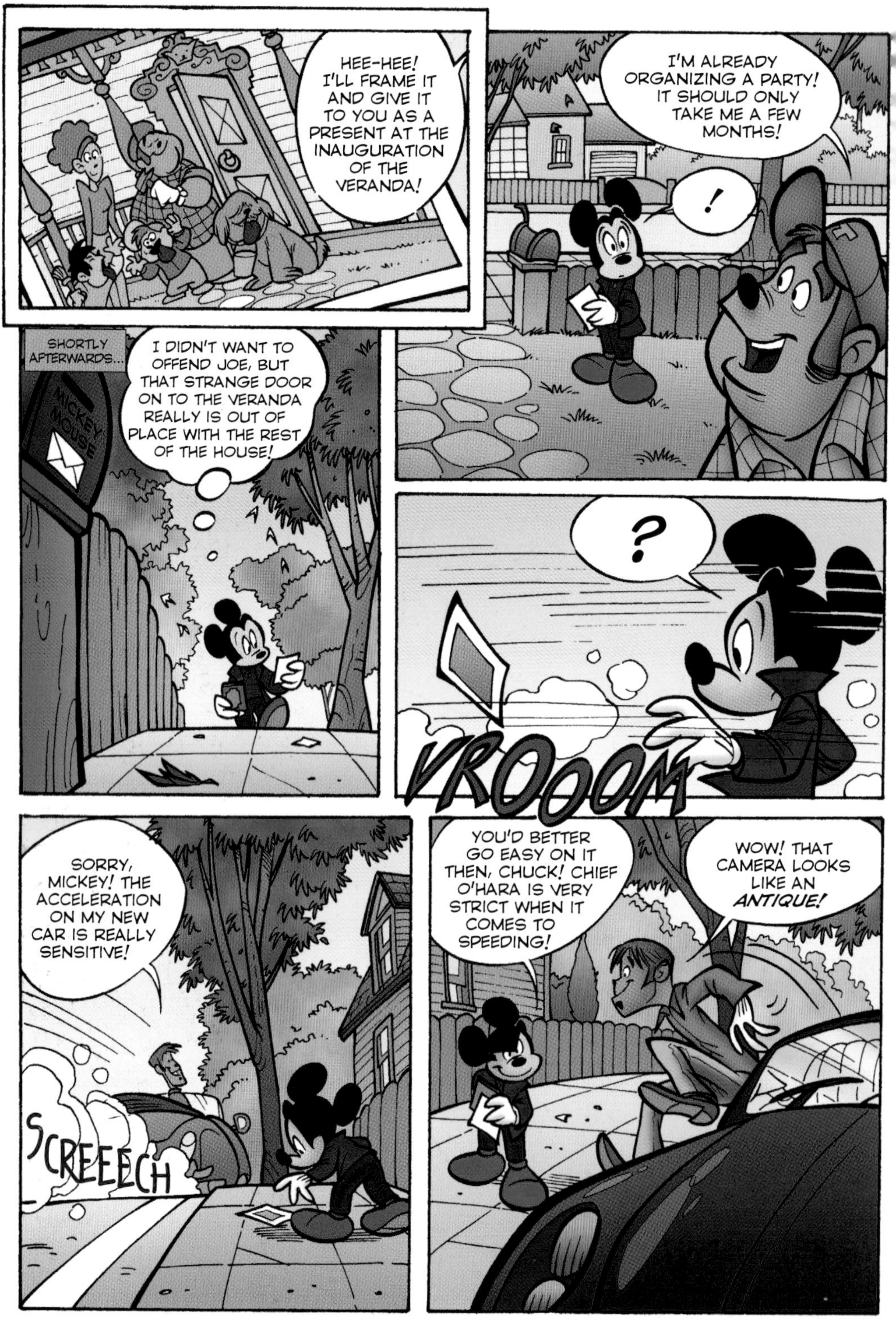
HEE-HEE! I'LL FRAME IT AND GIVE IT TO YOU AS A PRESENT AT THE INAUGURATION OF THE VERANDA!
I'M ALREADY ORGANIZING A PARTY! IT SHOULD ONLY TAKE ME A FEW MONTHS!
!
SHORTLY AFTERWARDS...
MICKEY MOUSE
I DIDN'T WANT TO OFFEND JOE, BUT THAT STRANGE DOOR ON TO THE VERANDA REALLY IS OUT OF PLACE WITH THE REST OF THE HOUSE!
?
VROOOOM
SORRY, MICKEY! THE ACCELERATION ON MY NEW CAR IS REALLY SENSITIVE!
SCREEECH
YOU'D BETTER GO EASY ON IT THEN, CHUCK! CHIEF O'HARA IS VERY STRICT WHEN IT COMES TO SPEEDING!
WOW! THAT CAMERA LOOKS LIKE AN *ANTIQUE!*

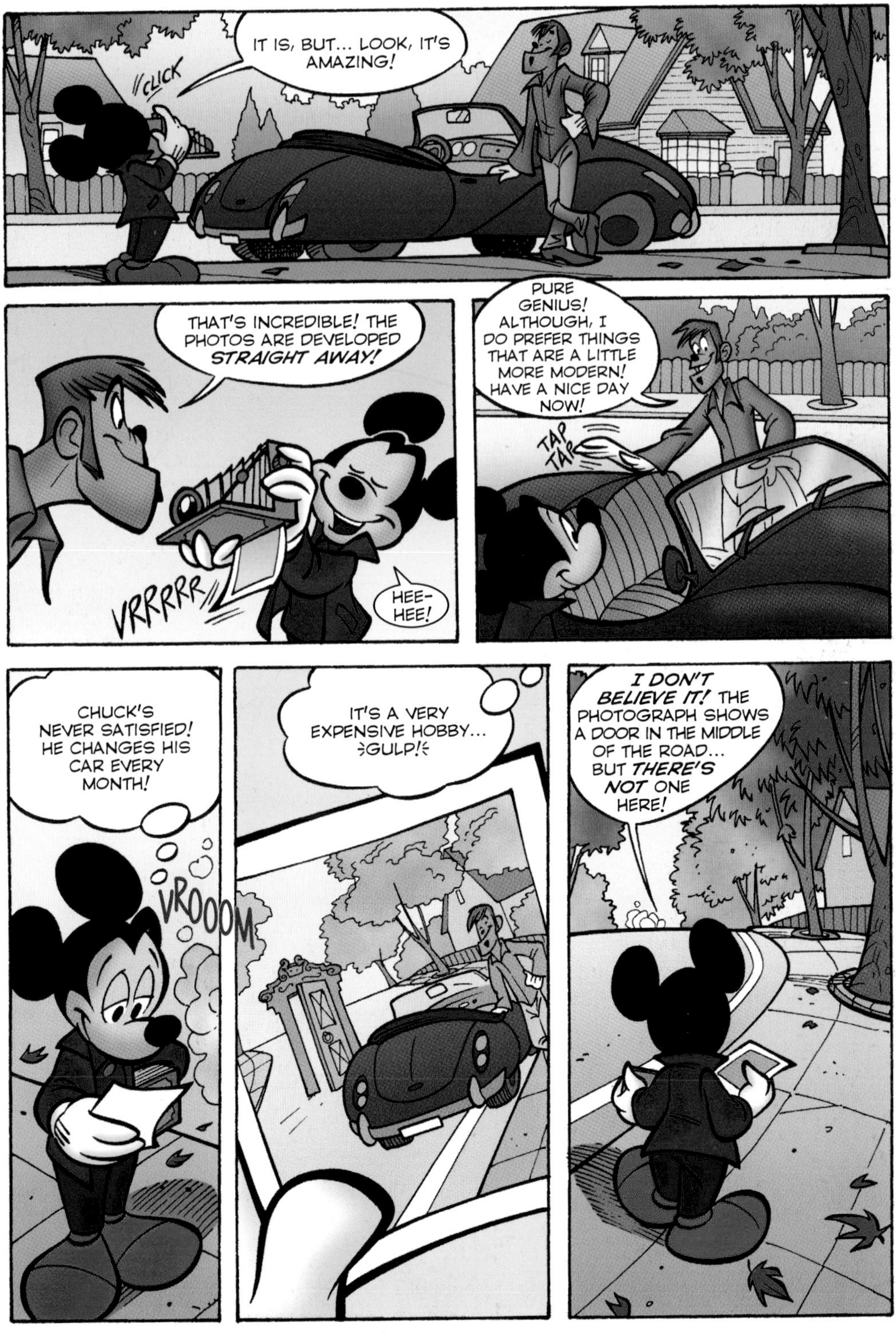
CLICK
IT IS, BUT... LOOK, IT'S AMAZING!
THAT'S INCREDIBLE! THE PHOTOS ARE DEVELOPED STRAIGHT AWAY!
VRRRRR
HEE-HEE!
PURE GENIUS! ALTHOUGH, I DO PREFER THINGS THAT ARE A LITTLE MORE MODERN! HAVE A NICE DAY NOW!
TAP TAP
CHUCK'S NEVER SATISFIED! HE CHANGES HIS CAR EVERY MONTH!
VROOOM
IT'S A VERY EXPENSIVE HOBBY... GULP!
I DON'T BELIEVE IT! THE PHOTOGRAPH SHOWS A DOOR IN THE MIDDLE OF THE ROAD... BUT THERE'S NOT ONE HERE!

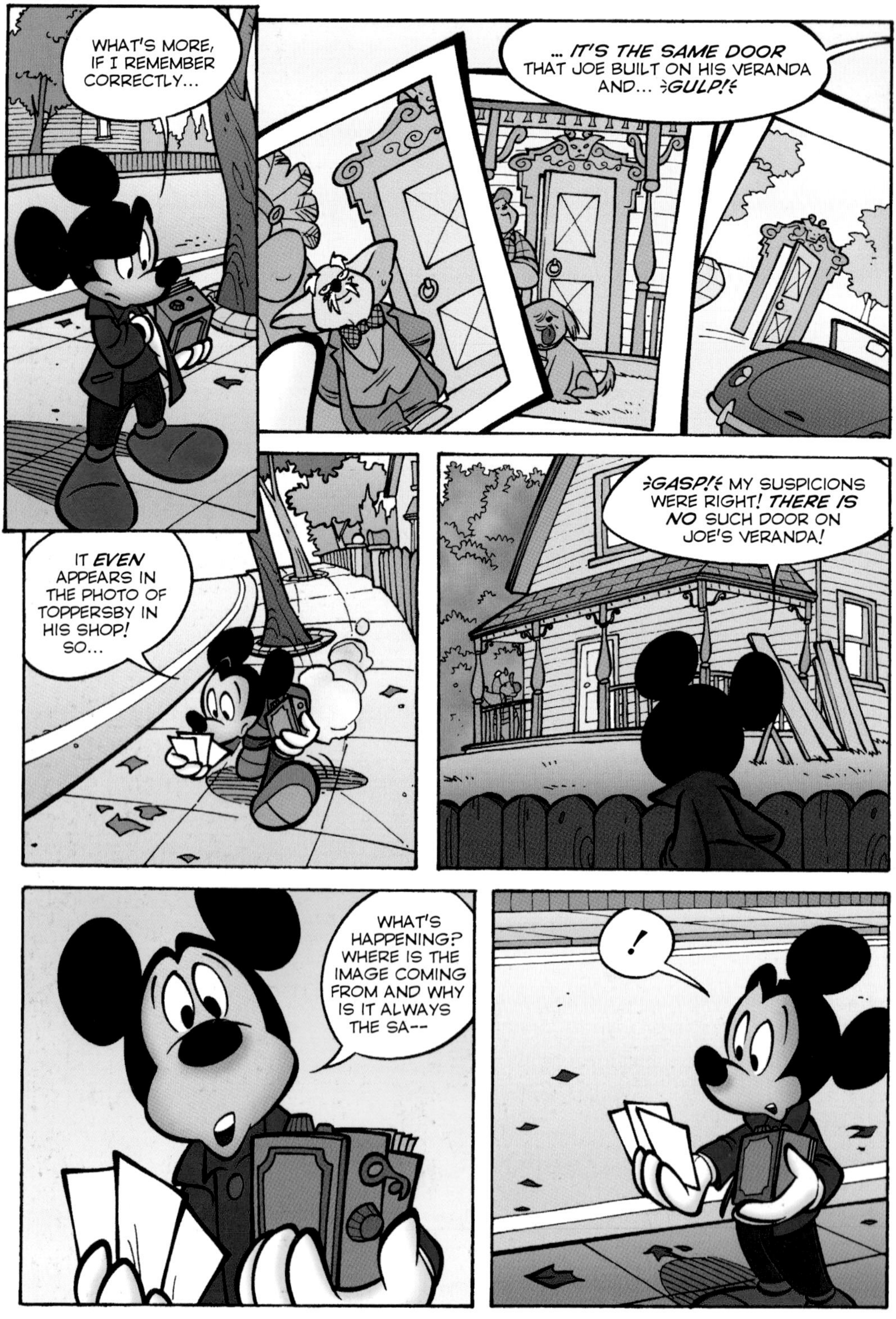
WHAT'S MORE, IF I REMEMBER CORRECTLY...
... IT'S THE SAME DOOR THAT JOE BUILT ON HIS VERANDA AND... GULP!
IT EVEN APPEARS IN THE PHOTO OF TOPPERSBY IN HIS SHOP! SO...
GASP! MY SUSPICIONS WERE RIGHT! THERE IS NO SUCH DOOR ON JOE'S VERANDA!
WHAT'S HAPPENING? WHERE IS THE IMAGE COMING FROM AND WHY IS IT ALWAYS THE SA--
!

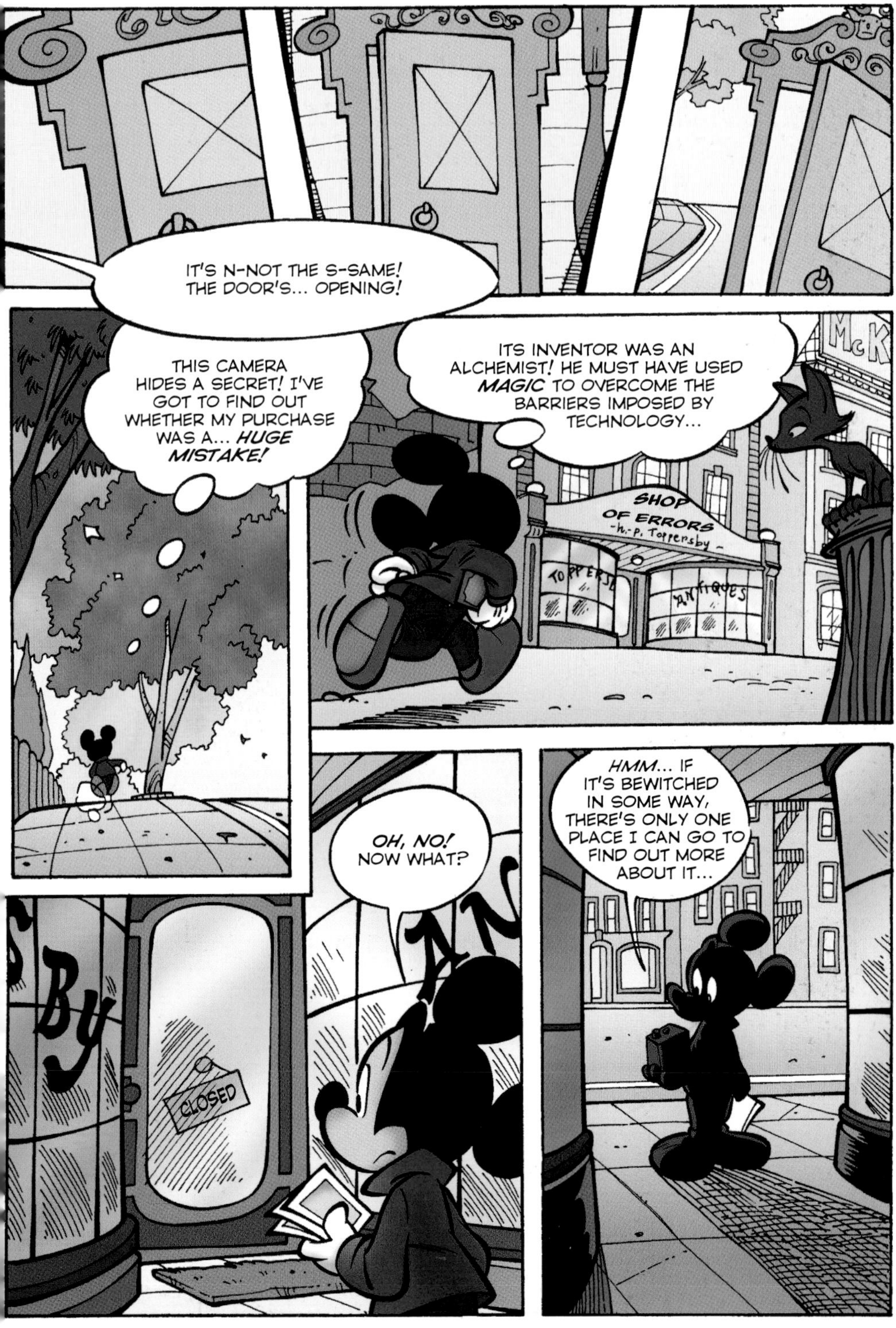
IT'S N-NOT THE S-SAME! THE DOOR'S... OPENING!
THIS CAMERA HIDES A SECRET! I'VE GOT TO FIND OUT WHETHER MY PURCHASE WAS A... HUGE MISTAKE!
ITS INVENTOR WAS AN ALCHEMIST! HE MUST HAVE USED MAGIC TO OVERCOME THE BARRIERS IMPOSED BY TECHNOLOGY...
SHOP OF ERRORS
-h.p. Toppersby -
TOPPERSB
ANTIQUES
OH, NO! NOW WHAT?
CLOSED
HMM... IF IT'S BEWITCHED IN SOME WAY, THERE'S ONLY ONE PLACE I CAN GO TO FIND OUT MORE ABOUT IT...

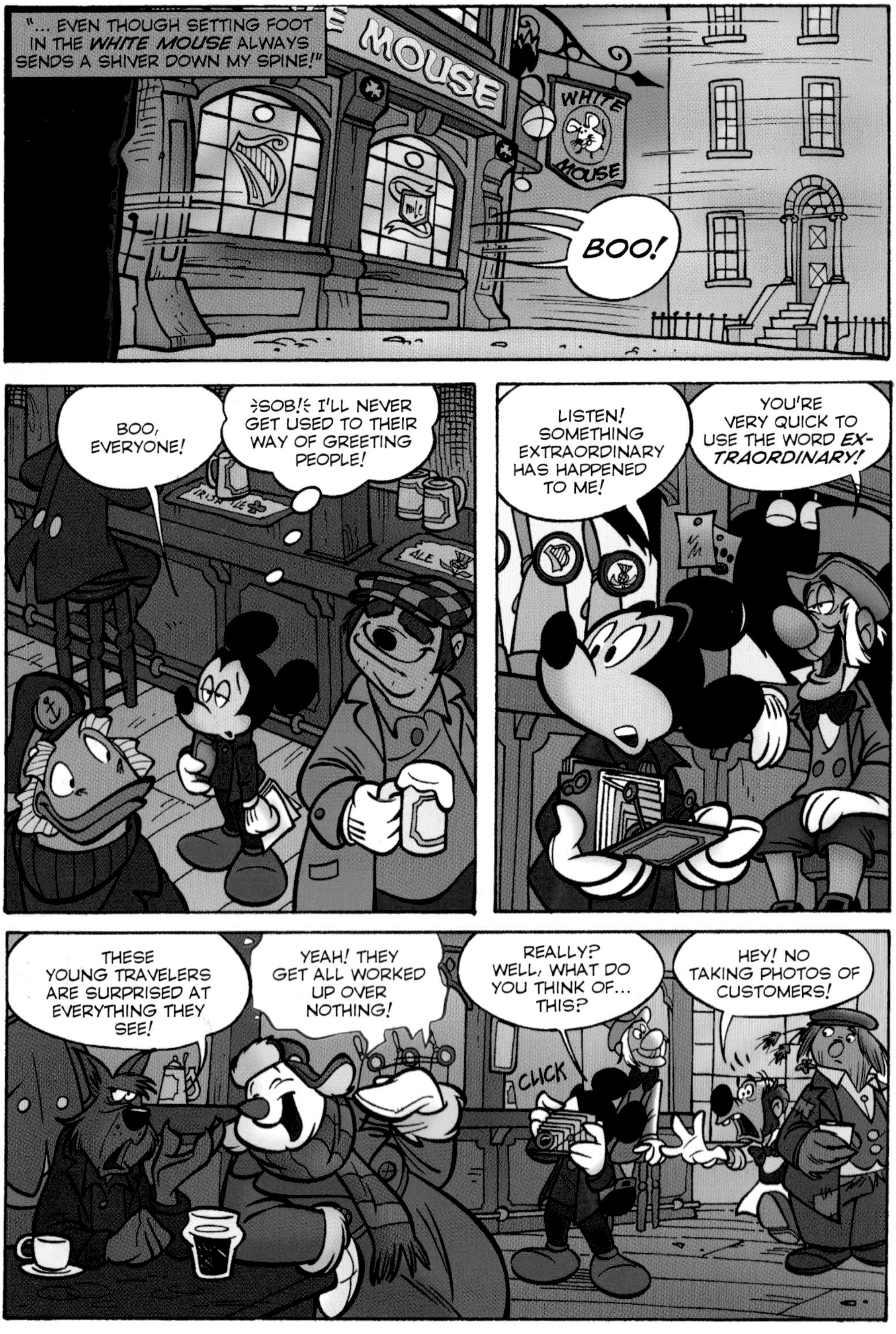
"... EVEN THOUGH SETTING FOOT IN THE *WHITE MOUSE* ALWAYS SENDS A SHIVER DOWN MY SPINE!"
MOUSE
WHITE MOUSE
BOO!
BOO, EVERYONE!
SOB! I'LL NEVER GET USED TO THEIR WAY OF GREETING PEOPLE!
LISTEN! SOMETHING EXTRAORDINARY HAS HAPPENED TO ME!
YOU'RE VERY QUICK TO USE THE WORD ***EXTRAORDINARY!***
THESE YOUNG TRAVELERS ARE SURPRISED AT EVERYTHING THEY SEE!
YEAH! THEY GET ALL WORKED UP OVER NOTHING!
REALLY? WELL, WHAT DO YOU THINK OF... THIS?
CLICK
HEY! NO TAKING PHOTOS OF CUSTOMERS!

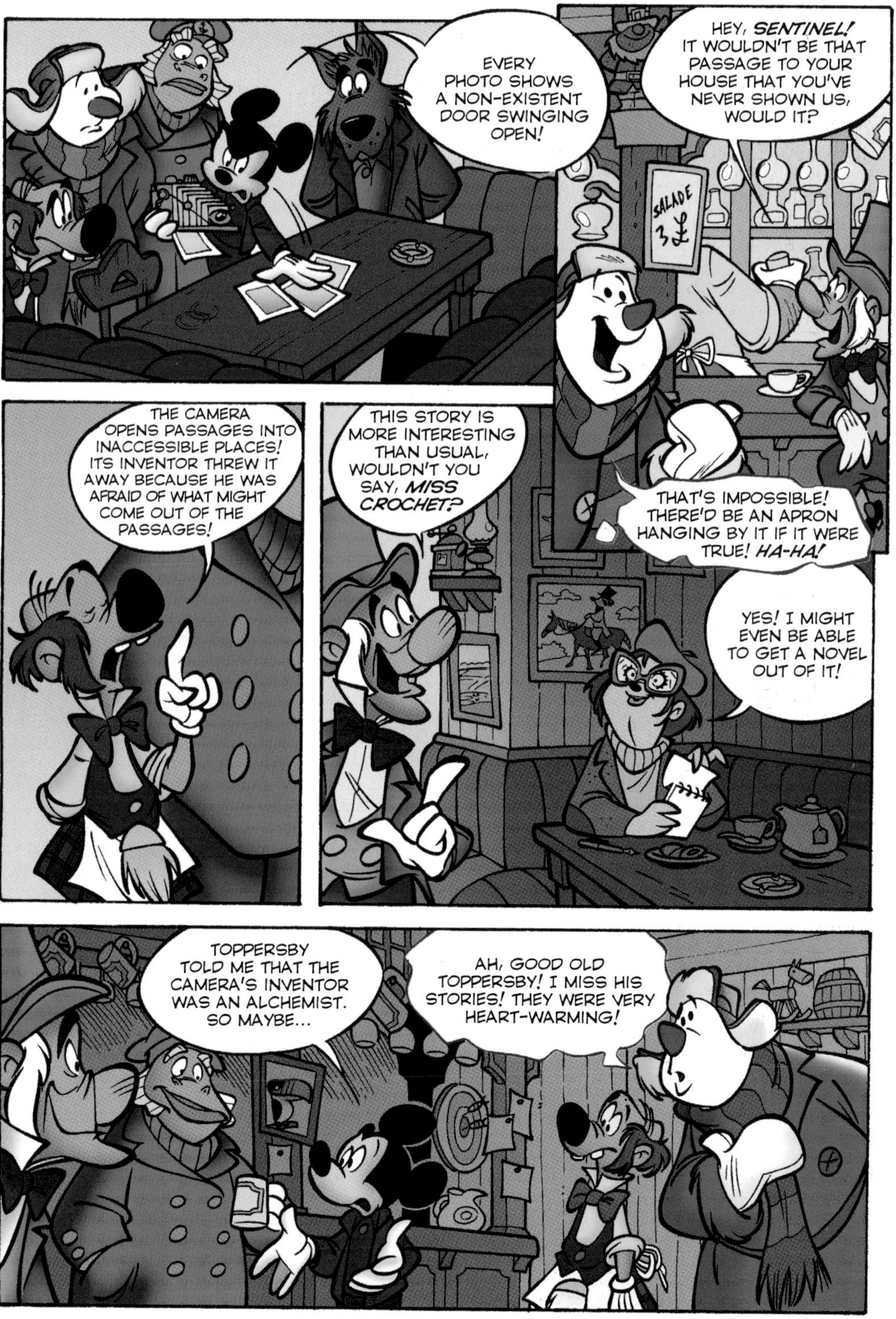
EVERY PHOTO SHOWS A NON-EXISTENT DOOR SWINGING OPEN!
HEY, SENTINEL! IT WOULDN'T BE THAT PASSAGE TO YOUR HOUSE THAT YOU'VE NEVER SHOWN US, WOULD IT?
THAT'S IMPOSSIBLE! THERE'D BE AN APRON HANGING BY IT IF IT WERE TRUE! HA-HA!
SALADE 3 £
THE CAMERA OPENS PASSAGES INTO INACCESSIBLE PLACES! ITS INVENTOR THREW IT AWAY BECAUSE HE WAS AFRAID OF WHAT MIGHT COME OUT OF THE PASSAGES!
THIS STORY IS MORE INTERESTING THAN USUAL, WOULDN'T YOU SAY, MISS CROCHET?
YES! I MIGHT EVEN BE ABLE TO GET A NOVEL OUT OF IT!
TOPPERSBY TOLD ME THAT THE CAMERA'S INVENTOR WAS AN ALCHEMIST. SO MAYBE...
AH, GOOD OLD TOPPERSBY! I MISS HIS STORIES! THEY WERE VERY HEART-WARMING!

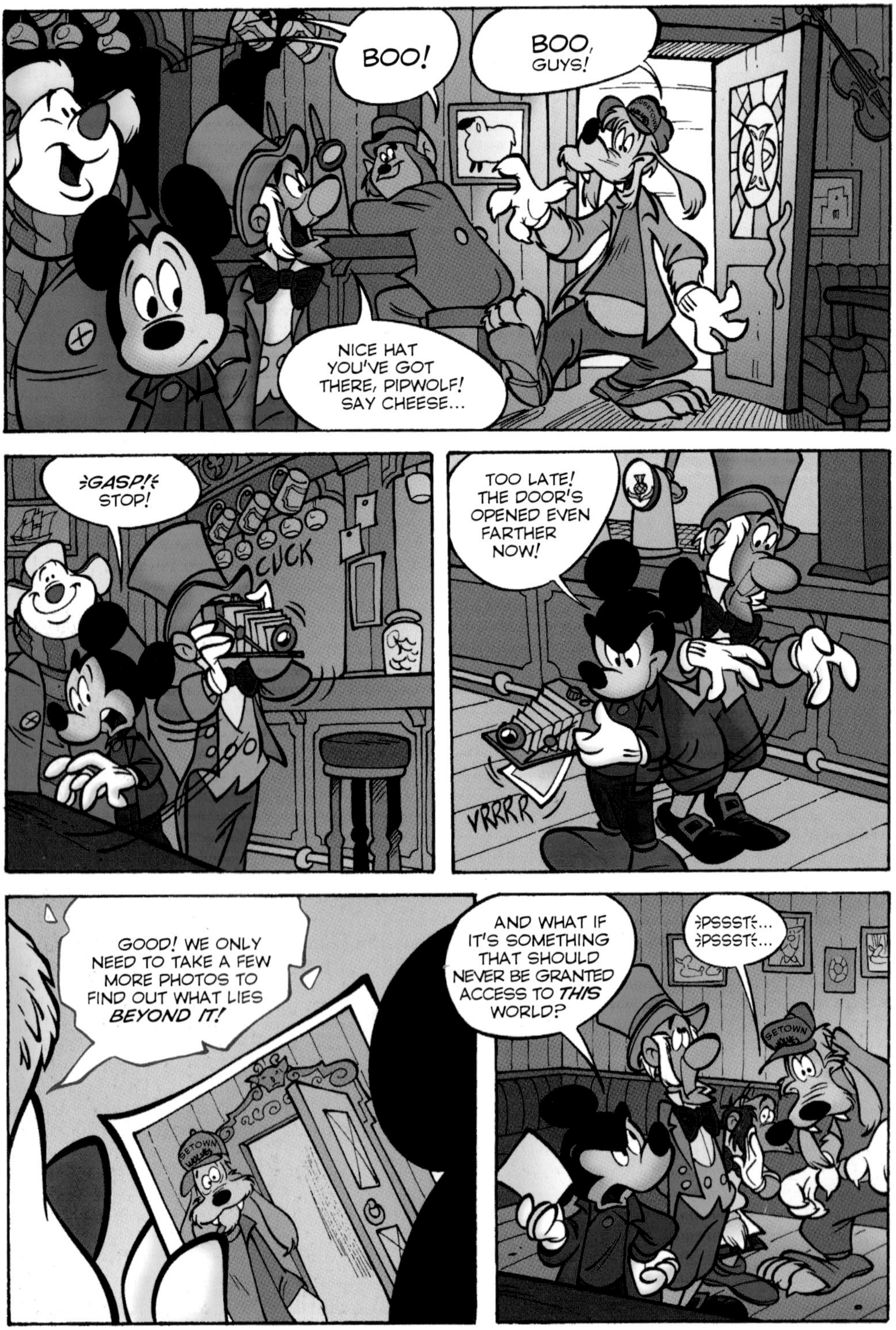
BOO!
BOO, GUYS!
NICE HAT YOU'VE GOT THERE, PIPWOLF! SAY CHEESE...
GASP! STOP!
CLICK
TOO LATE! THE DOOR'S OPENED EVEN FARTHER NOW!
VRRRR
GOOD! WE ONLY NEED TO TAKE A FEW MORE PHOTOS TO FIND OUT WHAT LIES *BEYOND IT!*
AND WHAT IF IT'S SOMETHING THAT SHOULD NEVER BE GRANTED ACCESS TO *THIS* WORLD?
PSSST... PSSST...

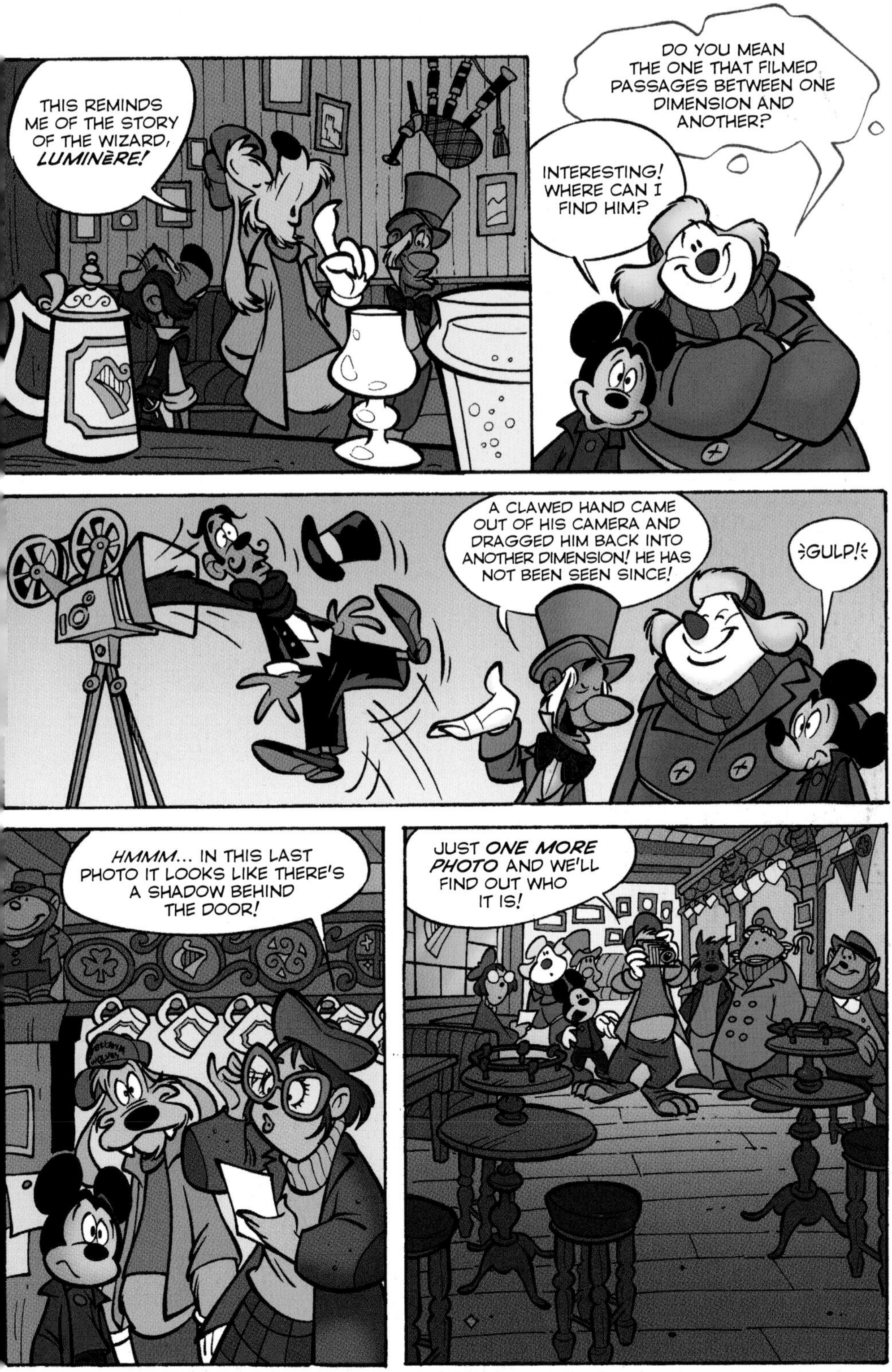
THIS REMINDS ME OF THE STORY OF THE WIZARD, *LUMINÈRE!*
DO YOU MEAN THE ONE THAT FILMED PASSAGES BETWEEN ONE DIMENSION AND ANOTHER?
INTERESTING! WHERE CAN I FIND HIM?
A CLAWED HAND CAME OUT OF HIS CAMERA AND DRAGGED HIM BACK INTO ANOTHER DIMENSION! HE HAS NOT BEEN SEEN SINCE!
GULP!
HMMM... IN THIS LAST PHOTO IT LOOKS LIKE THERE'S A SHADOW BEHIND THE DOOR!
JUST *ONE MORE PHOTO* AND WE'LL FIND OUT WHO IT IS!

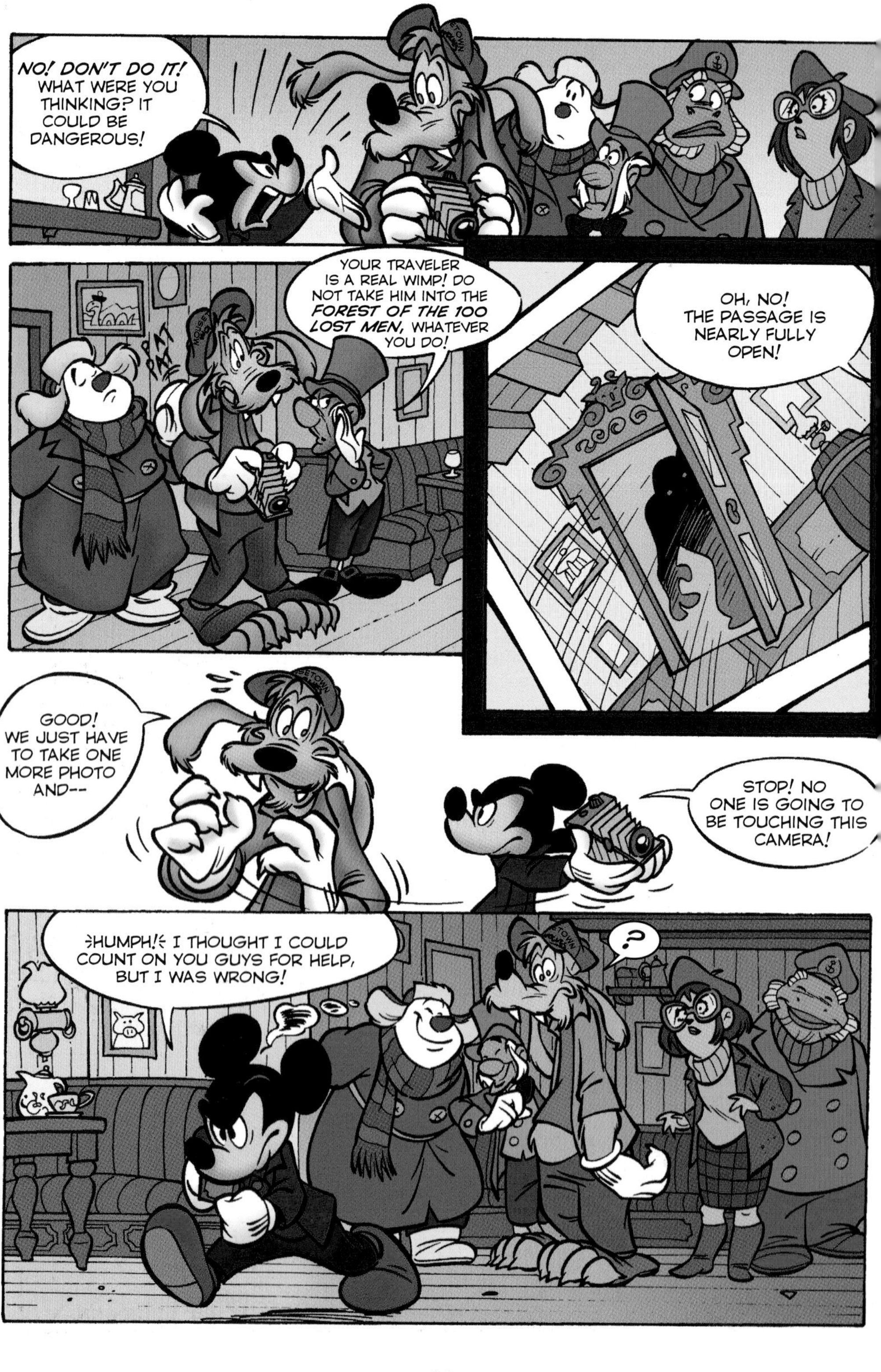
NO! DON'T DO IT! WHAT WERE YOU THINKING? IT COULD BE DANGEROUS!
YOUR TRAVELER IS A REAL WIMP! DO NOT TAKE HIM INTO THE FOREST OF THE 100 LOST MEN, WHATEVER YOU DO!
PAT PAT
OH, NO! THE PASSAGE IS NEARLY FULLY OPEN!
GOOD! WE JUST HAVE TO TAKE ONE MORE PHOTO AND--
STOP! NO ONE IS GOING TO BE TOUCHING THIS CAMERA!
HUMPH! I THOUGHT I COULD COUNT ON YOU GUYS FOR HELP, BUT I WAS WRONG!
?

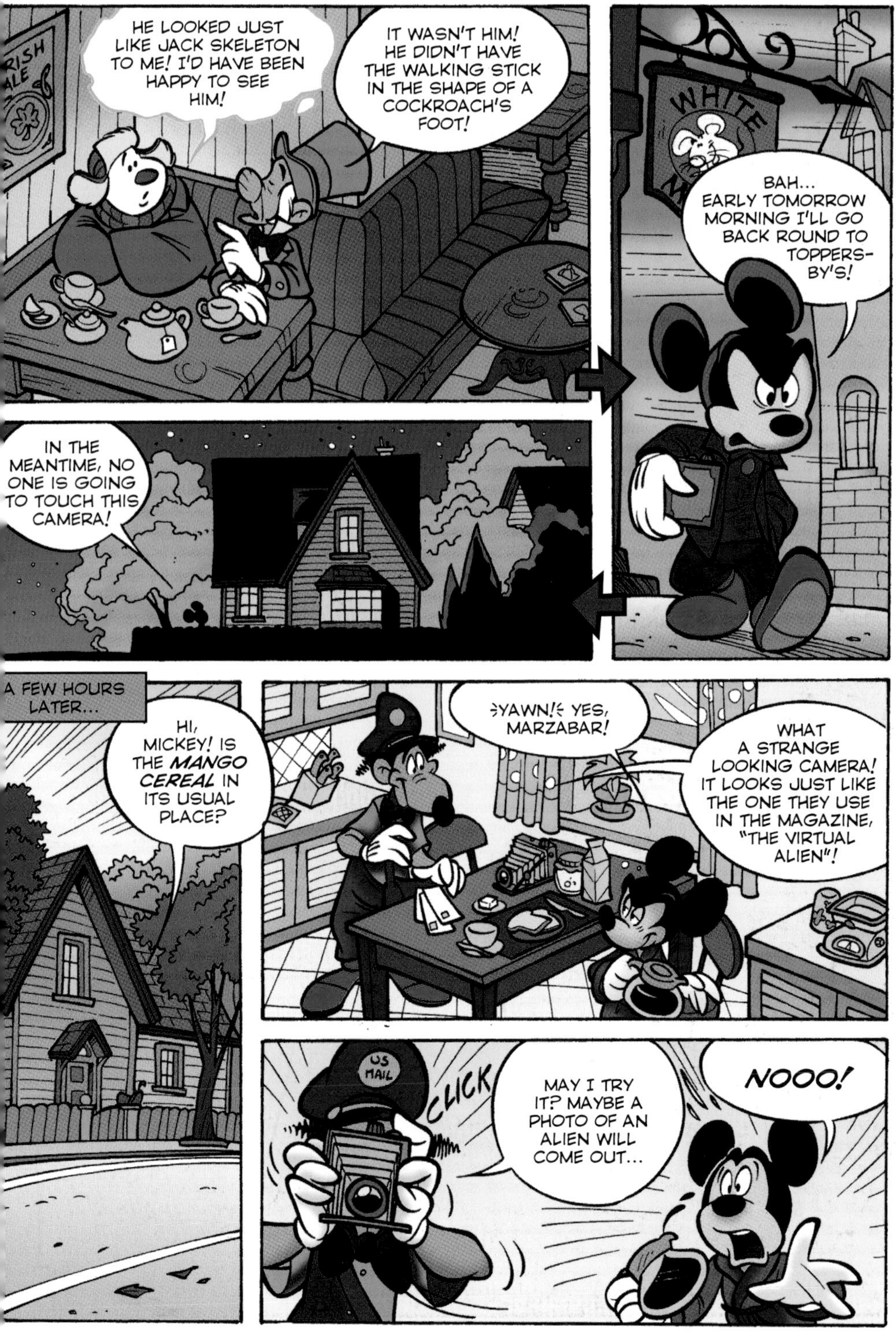
IRISH ALE
HE LOOKED JUST LIKE JACK SKELETON TO ME! I'D HAVE BEEN HAPPY TO SEE HIM!
IT WASN'T HIM! HE DIDN'T HAVE THE WALKING STICK IN THE SHAPE OF A COCKROACH'S FOOT!
WHITE
BAH... EARLY TOMORROW MORNING I'LL GO BACK ROUND TO TOPPERS-BY'S!
IN THE MEANTIME, NO ONE IS GOING TO TOUCH THIS CAMERA!
A FEW HOURS LATER...
HI, MICKEY! IS THE *MANGO CEREAL* IN ITS USUAL PLACE?
⇉YAWN!⇇ YES, MARZABAR!
WHAT A STRANGE LOOKING CAMERA! IT LOOKS JUST LIKE THE ONE THEY USE IN THE MAGAZINE, "THE VIRTUAL ALIEN"!
US MAIL
CLICK
MAY I TRY IT? MAYBE A PHOTO OF AN ALIEN WILL COME OUT...
NOOO!

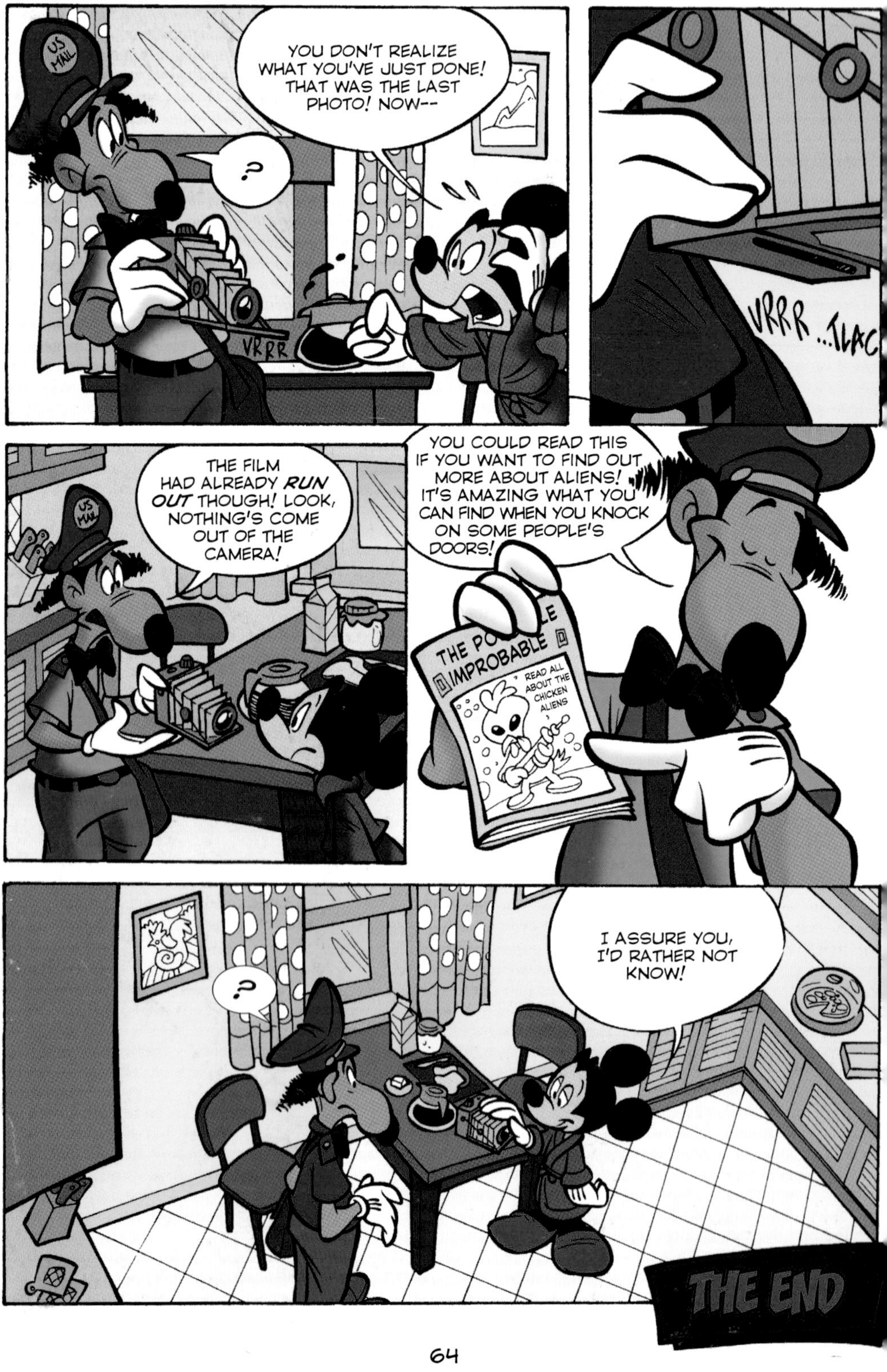
YOU DON'T REALIZE WHAT YOU'VE JUST DONE! THAT WAS THE LAST PHOTO! NOW--
?
VRRR
VRRR ...TLAC
THE FILM HAD ALREADY **RUN OUT** THOUGH! LOOK, NOTHING'S COME OUT OF THE CAMERA!
YOU COULD READ THIS IF YOU WANT TO FIND OUT MORE ABOUT ALIENS! IT'S AMAZING WHAT YOU CAN FIND WHEN YOU KNOCK ON SOME PEOPLE'S DOORS!
IMPROBABLE
READ ALL ABOUT THE CHICKEN ALIENS
?
I ASSURE YOU, I'D RATHER NOT KNOW!
THE END